# AS
# ITHACA
# LAY
# FORGOTTEN

# JONATHAN D. CLARK

## Also by Jonathan D. Clark

NOVELS
Division Street
In Perfect Lines
Arcadia
False Cathedrals

# About the author

Jonathan D. Clark (the writing pseudonym of Jourdan Dunn) was born in Redding, California, where he currently resides with his son. He published his debut novel, *Division Street*, in 2016. He is also the author of three other novels, including *Arcadia* and *False Cathedrals*.

author is a narcissistic gaslighting abuser
of women. Just FYI

AS ITHACA LAY FORGOTTEN

First Edition, 2022

Set in Electra

Cover & Interior Design by Jonathan D. Clark

Imprint: Independently Published

To Yvonne Daski

# AS ITHACA
# LAY FORGOTTEN

# CHAPTER 1

### LIKE EMPTY PAGES OF A NOVEL

# §1

## PARADISE

PAST A SEA OF WEATHERED PLAINS, beyond the height of forgotten grain towers and telephone poles long since out of commission, the quiet colors of the earth drifted in and out; a well-rehearsed routine. Warm splashes of amaranth and tangerine crossed paths at the fleeting shoreline of tired lavender, eager to greet the inevitable sway of indigo's morning reign. And all the tired urchins continued to sleep and dream, too stubborn to leave their self-contained world of make-believe.

It is a tapestry only the early bird sees.

With only the morning sun trailing behind him—his incandescent squire—Havoc had the highway all to himself, an endless network of faded paint and asphalt. Memories from his childhood gathered along the passing roadside, at the periphery of his already preoccupied mind. They were memories of him and his father traveling down the same stretch of road, of days and nights spent scouring every deserted metropolis they happened to come across on their never-ending journey to find a new place to call home; somewhere untouched by the winds of past destruction.

But they never found such a city.

Instead, they settled somewhere in the desert—an oasis of bright lights on the outskirts of town an everyday marvel when the sun fell beyond the horizon with reckless abandon; a far cry from their humble farmland origins.

"Are we almost there, Papa?" he would ask when they were traveling west, toward the coast; his small, frail voice barely audible above the roar of the car's diesel engine.

His father would simply turn his gaze to his son and smile before succumbing to a coughing fit. It wouldn't be until the end of the day when he would answer the question: "We still have a ways to go little one, but we'll get there eventually."

But the coughing only worsened as the days pressed on and the miles fell beneath their feet and disappeared behind them in the rearview mirror, their original town a distant memory.

So the city of lights became their home as his father's health continued to decline; the thought of one day continuing onward eventually became a fantasy. And when his old man passed away, months of suffering finally over, the earth went on without him and the highway lay forgotten.

For years Havoc couldn't bring himself to think about the memories he and his father had shared on the open road; they only reminded him of his situation—forced to live in the middle of the desert, surrounded by a family of outcasts who shared the misfortune of settling in such a barren landscape.

He promised himself he would leave when he got older, return to the asphalt sea and continue where he and his father left off when he was a small child, but he had grown comfortable in his imposed exile; here, in the small town of Paradise. That was the curse of small town living: one could easily find themselves convinced to stay there forever. Because even though the surrounding convenience stores were beginning to run low on canned food and the closest cattle ranch could no longer provide enough meat for trade, Paradise had become a part of Havoc's identity; its landmarks his playground, the people his family, and its irradiated skyline the canvas to his daydreams—an untouched safe haven surrounded by a world that had been completely obliterated at the hands of the Atom.

*There's no place like home,* he told himself as sun-bleached street signs and petrified cacti came and went on his way into the city.

HE ENJOYED DRIVING on the wrong side of the road whenever in the area. The look of discomposed horror among pedestrians and passing motorists humored him. "Look out, everyone. Havoc's in town." he would hear in the breeze, followed shortly by defensive horn blasts that begged him to get out of the way before they steered themselves clear of his unmoving path.

"You're going to kill someone one of these days," old man Ford said as he approached Havoc's vehicle once he parked along the sidewalk.

"I don't understand why you insist we continue to implement such archaic rules of the road," Havoc said, walking toward the front entrance of one of the city's bookstores. "The world went to hell æons ago. Why even bother keeping anything from that period of time? It's gone, forever a part of our past."

"And yet you continue to use a machine from that *lifetime* you'd rather forget in order to get around from place to place," Ford chuckled, amused. "And every week you drive over here to return your previous read to check out a new one. But why? Why not keep the books you take for your own and build a collection? There's no bookkeeper to stop you, nor is there a librarian to penalize you for a late return; yet you arrive here, every seventh day, at the break of dawn, like clockwork, to switch out novels, replenish your food supply, and top off your tank with peanut oil."

Ford turned his ancient gaze to watch as the city's residents left their respected shelters and carried on with their lives, doing their best to survive another day out in the Wasteland.

"Some things, Havoc, are worth keeping alive, even if they appear illogical to the eye of an outsider."

Havoc shrugged off Ford's words of sentiment and continued on his predetermined path into the bookstore's interior.

The old man followed.

It still fascinated him, the idea of a building that housed centuries of the written word—free to be absorbed by anyone who found solace in the silence of flipping through a novel's pages, the humdrum horrors of the real world tucked away for a couple of hours while they lost themselves in a world created from the imagination of an individual long gone; safe from ever having to experience the grim reality Havoc and the rest of the Earth's remaining population were forced to endure.

"Why do you read all these books, Havoc?" Ford asked, curious. "Nobody's forcing you to consume every word, every page."

"Do you ever wonder what life was like for people before it all went away?"

"All the time, without question; sometimes even when I sleep and a dream finds my tired brain. Images and other little reminders from the past that still linger fill my head with questions. I often wonder what a carpool lane signified—little mysteries left behind by our ancestors without context. But what does that have to do with reading all these works of fiction?"

"Honestly? I find it such a fascinating phenomenon," Havoc said as he walked down an aisle of titled spines. "The polarizing effect certain books can have on the reader. You can read two novels that tell a similar story, a tale of impending doom that rests on the horizon, and one will read as a hopeless forewarning, that if we continue down a certain path we'll be met with inevitable annihilation, while the other offers solutions for the narrative's cast—a voice of ambition which leans toward the preservation of man and the planet they call home. And sometimes these two separate pieces of literature can be written by the same author, at different periods of their life."

The room grew silent as Havoc continued to sort through each title, passing over every duplicate of a novel he had already read from previous visits. He wondered if Ford (or anyone else) had taken to reading to help pass the time. There wasn't much else to do in the desert, so it made sense that *someone else* would find the notion of consuming the written word worthwhile, if not entertaining; an easy way to spend a few hours of the day away from the derelict and hopeless view the real world had to offer them.

Ford sighed as he watched Havoc continue to scan the shelves of books. "If only they had the foresight to look for a solution that could have helped to prevent the world from ending the way it did."

"But that's the unfortunate truth with literature, I'm afraid," Havoc said, his eyes not missing a beat as they traveled down, row by row. "Even if the author stumbled upon such a solution, their cautionary tale would have lived on as nothing more than a *beautifully composed work of fiction*, and whatever message the writer wished to convey to their audience would've found itself lost somewhere on the page until the state of the world fell into every pitfall the novel warned against; our fate warped beyond repair."

"So you're saying we chose to remain ignorant?" Ford asked, a hint of solemnity in his voice.

"One might consider it 'plausible deniability' in the grand scheme of things," Havoc said. "After all, some would argue the point of the novel was to only entertain its intended audience and that any indication of deeper meaning had only been fabricated speculation brought forth by the reader."

"Remind me to never read *those* kind of books, should I ever find myself curious enough to take part in your little . . . hobby."

Havoc laughed as he reached over to grab a brick of a novel he had already read and handed it to the old man. "If you're wanting a lighter read, this is a good place to start."

Ford took the weight of the book in his hand; its heft unexpected, despite its thickness. He examined the paperback's worn exterior front to back. While already unsure how to properly pronounce the title, the blurb on the back of the book only served to confuse him more. His gaze shifted to Havoc, who was still looking for something new to take home with him for the coming week.

"You want me to believe this entire novel takes place in one day?"

"Why is that so hard to believe?"

"Look at the size of this thing!" Ford held the book out by its spine and let the pages flutter about haphazardly. "I mean, seriously. How much could happen in a single day?"

"You'd be surprised."


AFTER SCOURING THE BOOKSTORE'S SHELVES for what felt like an eternity, having finally settled on a new read for the upcoming week, Havoc and Ford left the shaded comfort of the bookstore.

"Why must you insist on living on the outskirts of town?" Ford asked as they stepped back into the heat. "I know things never felt the same after your old man passed away, but you've always been welcome to live here with the rest of us. There's still plenty of room. You could bunk with Gillette at the movie theater. I'm sure she wouldn't mind seeing you again."

"I don't know about living here again," Havoc said as they made their way toward his car to find little Bronco (Ford's grandson) wiping the sweat from his brow as he finished topping off the fuel tank, Havoc's usual order of supplies resting neatly on the back seat. "But I guess I could stop by the cineplex on my way out to say hello; catch up and all that."

"She asks about you every week when you drop by for supplies, minutes after you've left. She misses you, you know. The two of you used to be such good friends. Hell, I can't even remember a moment you two were ever apart growing up."

Havoc looked up toward the sun, its warm presence looming overhead. With only the drive home left in his day to consider, he figured he could afford the detour for an hour or two. After all, what harm could come from visiting an old friend?

# §2

## SILENT CINEMA

NLIKE EVERY OTHER BUILDING in the city of Paradise, the movie theater's outer appearance was anything but unassuming; its square-faced marquee and towering light fixture a clear standout among the sea of small town architecture. And as Havoc stepped through the double front doorway, its wooden doors left unlocked and ajar during the day, he felt nostalgia envelop his senses: the smell of the building's dust-covered wood paneling, the untouched popcorn machine still a technological marvel to his eyes, and the natural silence of the building's interior calmed him.

Fond memories from his childhood played on an endless loop, both comforting and haunting him at the same time. They reminded him that, despite his father's passing, life still had its beautiful moments. He wished he could go back. But unfortunately, he knew it to be an impossibility—that time could only travel forward and the simplicity of his childhood would remain lost to the past.

A noise echoed from above in one of the projection booths. A wry smile edged its way to Havoc's lips, knowing the sound well enough; still familiar to his ears after all these years. Somewhere on the second floor, Gillette and her mother could be heard prepping one of the still working devices so Gillette could watch her noonday film. He wondered why she still bothered with such relics. When they were kids any movie they watched had already lost a good portion of its original sound quality and certain scenes had shown visible signs of fading. By now he assumed watching a reel would be more a mess of empty framework and tortured static, with only the occasional echo of a character's once high-spirited dialogue bleeding through the speakers, than an actual motion picture.

Still, it warmed his heart to see some things had stayed the same, even after he left. And if memory served him well, he knew she would come running down the stairs and across the hallway so she wouldn't miss more than twenty seconds of the upcoming attractions.

"It's nice to know some things haven't changed around here," he yelled into the building's interior, making his presence known.

The sound of footsteps slowed to a halt for a brief moment before picking back up at a slower pace.

"Havoc? Is that you?" a voice echoed. But before he could answer, Gillette appeared from around the corner.

As always, she wore her hair up in a controlled mess with an amber hair clip her mother had given her, and she adorned herself with a faded band tee and a denim skirt with a flannel wrapped around her waist. And were she to have met him outside, he presumed she would have strapped on her leather combat boots to complete the ensemble.

"What brings you into the cineplex?" she said as she stepped down the small incline that led from the lobby and into the dimly lit hallway of auditoriums.

"What, no hello?"

"You normally just grab your supplies and hightail on out of here without missing a beat."

"Maybe I wanted to see how you were doing."

Gillette laughed. "You've never been one to let sincerity dictate your actions, so don't kid yourself. What really brings you in here?"

A silence developed. He understood her cynicism. Not a word had been exchanged between the two since he left for the outskirts of town four years ago. No explanation had been given as to why he left. But despite this understanding, it still hurt that she questioned his motivation for coming inside the theater

"Fine. You don't have to tell me," she said, putting an end to the quiet moment. "We can always come back to that later. But if you'd like to join me for a couple of hours, mother and I just finished setting up my first film of the day."

"I'm surprised they still work."

"They work well enough to pass the time. Now c'mon, we've already missed the first preview, and probably part of the second."


TOGETHER THEY SAT IN HUSHED TRANQUILITY as the projector illuminated the vinyl screen, the only source of light in the room. And just as Havoc had predicted, the condition of the reel had reached a point of decay beyond coherence. If Gillette could still find enjoyment with each viewing, it must've stemmed from her own recollection of the film's original lifespan. Because beyond the occasional flicker of an image and a never-ending rain of static, the movie had become unwatchable. But when Havoc looked over to Gillette, he noticed the same sense of wonderment in her eyes from when they were kids. It amused him, to bear witness to such an event. The film itself now a pale imitation of what it had been when it was first developed still managed to hold her attention. And even though the dialogue had become incoherent chatter, she quoted all her favorite moments as each actor's lips mouthed their rehearsed lines.

While he had never read the same book twice, Havoc considered his fascination with the written word a blessing. Because should he ever feel the desire to revisit a past read in the future, the condition of the novel would (he theorized) remain untouched by the passing of time; something he couldn't say for Gillette's love of cinema; eventually, she would find herself left with nothing but an empty screen and she would have to rely solely on her memory to keep it all alive.

"Why do you keep watching these?" he asked. "If all you end up seeing is a clear image every few minutes, with a distorted soundbite here and there, why even bother?"

"I like to think of this as time travel," she said. Her eyes remained locked on the screen, mesmerized by every fleeting image. "If only for a minute or two, my mind will wander off; it'll find itself transported to whenever these films were made. Life seemed easy then. You could lose yourself in a beautiful moment and stay there for a while; let it consume you. Two strangers could enjoy a night out in an unfamiliar town. You could fall in love with someone you just met, even if the odds were stacked against you—that you would only have the *one night* together. It's inspiring."

Gillette's words sat with him for a bit while the movie continued to play. He turned his attention toward the screen and caught a moment where the film's reel hadn't been entirely erased. He could see the two main characters walking through the city of Vienna, enjoying the act of getting to know one another. And it was here that Havoc would shamelessly admit film's superiority over literature. Where one could only imagine the beauty of the world presented in the novel (entirely reliant on the author's ability to paint with words), a motion picture actually took place in such breathtaking environments. You could find yourself inhabiting the world's landscape displayed on the screen before you and get lost in the details as they passed by.

"Do you ever think about leaving?"

Havoc's gaze returned to Gillette to find her attention now rested on him.

"What do you mean?" he asked. "You mean leave Paradise? Sure, all the time."

"Why haven't you?"

"My dad died. We were supposed to just pass through here, but he got sick and . . . well, you know."

"But that was so many years ago."

"I don't understand."

"You're a bit older now, capable of going out and making it on your own. Why haven't you?"

He couldn't answer her. He didn't have a reason suitable enough to use that would explain why he chose to stay, despite having the ability to leave whenever he wanted.

"Havoc?"

"Gill?"

"Why haven't you left?"

"Do you want me to?"

"I didn't say that."

"Because it sounds like you want me to."

"It's just . . ." She paused and turned her head toward the screen, looking for the right words to say. "You always talked about leaving Paradise when you got older, back when we were kids. And then you left to live on the outskirts of town four years ago. Every week, when you would drive in for supplies and a new book, I always expected each visit to be your last before you made your grand departure. And every time you left, even though it was only to head back to your homestead, I'd find myself upset that you didn't make a pit stop to say goodbye. I mean, we shared a bedroom for Christ's sake. If you were to ever leave for good, I'd hope you'd at least come to say goodbye to me before heading out."

"Who knows if I ever will," he said.

"You owe it to yourself. Even if you end up coming back, a little time away from this place couldn't hurt."

"You just want me gone," Havoc said with a smirk.

Gillette smacked her friend across the shoulder. "I do not! Hell, if you do end up going on a trip, I'll be jealous the entire time you're gone. And of course I'll be begging you for details the moment you come back."

"*If* I come back."

"You better," Gillette said with a laugh. "I'd hate to have to break in a new best friend. You were hard enough as it was."

"You wouldn't have much to pick from in this town," Havoc said smiling. "I grew up in Paradise as well, remember? I know what's out there. If you and I were to leave ourselves out of the equation, it'd pretty much be a downhill slope from there on out."

The two shared a moment of playful hysterics before the room fell silent again. But he didn't mind the quiet. The air in the room reminded him of a time when they were still children, more occupied with running through the theater as they played a game of Hide and Seek with Gillette's mother while her father tended to the building's upkeep; his adopted family. They were inseparable in their youth. The disconnect between them had been sudden; unannounced. When Gillette's father had taken ill it reminded him too much of his own father's demise and he chose to remove himself from the environment. And while the man wasn't his flesh and blood, Havoc couldn't bring himself to watch another person close to him fall apart and become one more victim claimed by the elements of the Wasteland.

They spent the rest of the movie without a word mentioned between them. Even when the film went completely silent, with only the sound of the projector spinning tape from one end of the machine to the next, they refused to speak. Together they sat and admired what used to be present and alive on screen but had long since faded into nothingness, like empty pages of a novel. And where the absence of forward momentum would have bothered a casual viewer, a faithful admirer of the art of cinema had learned to appreciate the subtle nuances each frame of white noise continued to carry with it; its boundless potential. Because over time, as the memory of certain scenes lost their visual impact, leaving only an emotional imprint of how the movie made the person feel, their unreliable sense of recollection would (in the end) allow them to rewrite certain moments; the final result would remain the same, of course, but the journey leading to such a catharsis would (undoubtedly) be slightly different every time.

"Care to watch another one with me?"

From the faint glow of the silver screen Havoc caught the hopeful glimmer of Gillette's golden green eyes, a stark contrast against her honey-toned skin. He remembered the first time he saw them outside in the sun, how they appeared full of life. Such vibrancy carried itself, even in the darkness of the auditorium. His mind fell back to reality for a second, knowing he would have to leave soon if he wanted to make it home before sundown—when the creatures of the night awoke from their slumber to feed on anything (or anyone) unfortunate enough to find itself caught out in the wilderness.

But he couldn't bring himself to say no.

"Okay, but just one more," he said.


THE TOWN'S WARNING BELL started to ring just as their final motion picture came to a close; Gillette had talked him into a third. It would be dark soon and Havoc feared he missed his window to leave, that he wouldn't make it to safety before nightfall.

"Shit! Is it really almost sunset?" he asked, a nervous energy apparent in his voice.

"That's my fault," an apologetic Gillette said as they both stood from their seats. "I insisted we watch another after the shoot 'em up movie you like so much. Ever since that raid when we were kids, I can't do firearms all that well. I still have nightmares about that night every now and then."

"No, it's my fault. I should have remembered the sound of a gunfight would bother you."

"I should have talked you out of it. But since it had been a while since you've had some *decent entertainment* in your life, I wanted to treat you to something special—a childhood favorite."

"I should probably go soon. It's only going to get darker."

"Don't be ridiculous," Gillette grabbed Havoc by the hand and led him out of the darkness of the theater and into the hallway. "You can stay here for the night. It'll be like old times."

Havoc wanted to object to his friend's offer, but he made the mistake of (once again) staring into her eyes.

# §3

## LATE-NIGHT REFLECTIONS

**W**ITH THEIR ROOM DIMLY LIT by a small circle of candles, their minds unable to find rest, Havoc and Gillette sat and listened to the clandestine horrors that wandered the streets of Paradise under the moon's pale dominion. Shadows danced across the walls and ceiling as the world outside sang of unfathomable nightmares. And just as it had been when they were tireless adolescents, while the tortured sounds of wildlife occupied the midnight air, despite her father's insistence they remain quiet until sunrise, they allowed their restless thoughts fill the room.

"Have you ever wondered?"

"Wondered about what?" a confused Havoc's gaze drifted from the ceiling to meet Gillette's, the light from the candles having cast a subdued gloom underneath her cheekbones.

"I don't know," Gillette continued, now feeling hesitant—unsure of the direction she wanted to travel down. It had been a while since they last had a late-night conversation. "Do you . . . I mean . . . have you ever wondered what the world would be like today, had humanity not blown the entire planet to shit?"

"Who's to say it was the *entire* planet?"

"You think there were areas left untouched by the Atom?"

"Maybe not entirely. For example, look at Paradise. The town's infrastructure—for the most part—has remained intact, so whatever amount of radiation poisoning that managed to find itself in the air, ground, and water had to've carried itself on the wind from a nearby metropolis that had been hit full-on by an atomic detonation."

"Yeah, I guess that's true."

"And who knows, it's possible there could be a town out there somewhere that's completely unaware of the terrible fate the rest of the earth faced centuries ago."

"But what if the bombs *never* fell? Where do you think the world would be today, had we managed to refrain from acting on our violent impulses?"

"If some of the books I've read are any indication, we'd be living on the moon and several other planets by now."

"Other worlds, you say? Sounds fascinating. It's too bad those realities are nothing but the work of someone's imagination."

"What about you?"

"Hm?"

"What do you think the world would be like, had we not destroyed each other?"

"I'm sure the world would still have its problems, but I feel it would be a rather pleasant place to live in and explore, despite it all."

Havoc couldn't help but laugh.

"What?"

"A little optimistic, don't you think?"

"I don't think so."

"You truly believe that?"

"Well, why not? Is it wrong to believe that, if we had somehow managed to look past our differences and political rivalries, humanity could have created a better world for future generations?"

"Take a look around us, Gill. You don't have to go far to see the world is in complete shambles, has been for God knows how long, and we have yet to recover from it."

"Like you're one to talk," Gillette said, venom in her tone. "You have the nerve to sit there and criticize my reasonably upbeat theory on where we would be in an alternate timeline, yet you talk about people living on the moon and other planets. If you're looking to call an idea delusional, look no further than the books you've read during your self-imposed solitude."

The room went quiet, and the sounds from the outside world grew louder to fill the void. An unresolved tension existed between the two of them; they couldn't avoid it. Regret turned Havoc's stomach, knowing his words had stung. He didn't mean to insult Gillette's playful fantasy. After all, they were speaking in hypotheticals not to be taken seriously—passing the time before they fell asleep for the night.

But Gillette's feelings were justified. He had no right to criticize her account of what the world would be like when his sounded more far-fetched upon closer analysis. Even when humanity had managed to make their way to other planets, their own hubris would eventually destroy them by the end of the novel.

"Where would you go?" Gillette's voice broke the silence.

"What?"

"If you decided to leave one day, where would you go?"

"Originally, my father and I were heading west toward the coast. I don't believe the old man ever had a planned destination in mind when we set off. I can still remember the day we left my hometown behind. The details aren't one hundred percent clear, but you never really forget the day your mother died. Fragments of distant memory never truly leave you, do they—much like those films we enjoyed watching all the time as kids. The visual may fade and our ability to recall the movie shot for shot may deteriorate over time, but you never forget the basic story; you remember how it made you feel the first time you watched it on the big screen. It stays with you . . . forever. I remember seeing my mother off in the distance one minute as she tended to the field. And the next, a flash of white light rose from the earth and reached for the heavens, followed by a cloud of fire and twisted metal. It didn't take long for my father to come running into the house to collect me, carry me to the car, and leave. And all along the way, right up until we made it to Paradise, he continued to reassure me she didn't feel a thing when it happened."

From the other side of the room, Gillette's composure sank. She never knew the story of Havoc's mother, only that she wasn't with them when he and his father first arrived, and it pained her to hear him tell the tale in such an affectless tone.

"But," Havoc continued, "to answer the question: if I did decide to leave one day, I'd probably continue where my father and I left off and head for California. I doubt there's really anything left to see out there, since both the west and east coast got hit pretty hard, but it would be nice to finish what my father started—finally fulfill a promise I made."

Gillette's composure sank even further. "Well," she said with a pause, the words caught in her throat, "if you do decide to go, just know you will be missed. Fuck, I miss you already and you're only a fifteen minute drive away."

"You could always come visit me, you know," Havoc scoffed at her last remark. "It's not like you don't know where I live."

"Shut up!" Gillette said, throwing her pillow at her friend. "You of all people should know I don't have a car, and a fifteen minute drive translates into two hours if you're walking."

"Excuses," Havoc said with a smile. "And thanks for the pillow, by the way. You can never have too many."

"The point was: I'll miss you."

"Come with me."

"What?"

"If I leave for California, come with me."

"You can't be serious."

"But what if I am?"

"In a heartbeat, yes; I would go with you."

"Don't sound too excited."

"I know you're not serious, so I'm not going to get my hopes up. But if you were, I'm not going to deny my desire to go. We grew up on cinema, so to be able to visit the place where movies were made? the only question left is: When?"

Havoc's attention turned to the circle of candles, entranced by their dancing flames. The thought of leaving Paradise, saying farewell to the sense of security and routine it offered for the mysteries of the road, terrified him. Though he often daydreamed of returning to the highway—waking at the break of dawn so he could race the sun across the Interstate, to the other end of the horizon—for sixty-one seasons, he had called Paradise his home. But as he watched the candles continue to light the room, their alabaster existence dwindling by the minute, they reminded him how fleeting life could be. In one lifetime he had already lost his mother and two father figures, his own time on earth a fragile momentary lapse in reason.

"How does the day after tomorrow sound?"

"What are you on about now?" Gillette whined, half asleep.

Havoc smiled and told her they would talk about it more tomorrow morning, when they could go more in-depth on the details. Ready to call it a night himself, he blew out the candles and let the weight of sleep carry his mind elsewhere—to dream of the future.

# §4

# FAREWELL & DEPARTURE

REMNANTS OF LAST NIGHT'S DREAM carried a sliver of candid optimism into the Nevadan skyline, to welcome a new day with the morning sun. And even though the finer details had lost themselves to a fog upon awakening, Havoc woke up feeling hopeful for the first time in years.

A sense of excitement filled the room shortly after Gillette shook the leftover somnolence from her psyche.

Together they prepared for the trip ahead of them, unsure what to expect when they reached their final destination. While Gillette dreamed of visiting the City of Angels (where many of her favorite films were written, shot, and premiered to thunderous applause and spectacle), Havoc's focus rested on walking alongside the coastal waves of the Pacific Ocean as they ebbed and flowed without interruption—to feel the sand drift beneath his feet as it hitched a ride on the receding, effervescent tide.

"I don't know how I feel about all this," Ford said as he helped pack a week's worth of food into the trunk of Havoc's car. "I mean, it's one thing for *you* to drive out to the Californian Wasteland. But to take Gillette with you? I don't know if her father would've approved of such an idea."

"Well then it's a good thing he isn't here to object. Besides, she's an adult now—fully capable of making her own decisions. After all, it was her idea. Well, sort of. She said she wants to go, so I'm bringing her with me."

"What do you two even expect to find out there anyway? You've heard the stories. There's nothing but desolation out that way. And you run the risk of stumbling upon a camp of drifters who'd kill you both where you stand without hesitation and take all you had for themselves." Ford pulled Havoc close. "If you're going to head out west, I suggest you take this."

The old man handed him a revolver and leather holster. They looked similar to the ones he had seen in the Western he grew up watching and watched yesterday with Gillette. The weight of the weapon alone astonished him. How anyone could carry such an item with ease (let alone take aim and fire at their intended target) left him bemused. But once its leaden heft became less of a burden, he pointed it toward the sky and pulled the hammer back.

"The damned thing don't carry a lot when it comes to ammunition," Ford continued, handing him a box of bullets. "Only six slugs, unfortunately. But if you're able to get a couple of shots off before they do, I've heard they'll back off and leave you alone."

*The gunfight is in the head, not the hands*, Havoc thought, remembering one of his favorite lines from last night's shoot 'em up flick. And with a childlike grin, he pulled the trigger and let the hammer click against the firing pin in a harmless fashion.

"I figured if we keep to the main road we shouldn't have a problem with the likes of them," he said as he lowered the six shooter and admired its construction. It rested in his hands with such ease. His eyes traced every detail, the firearm's framework carried a mysticism with it; an unexplained marvel. "But if it makes you feel better about letting us leave, I'll keep it on me at all times."

"Nothing is going to make me feel *better* about you leaving," Ford said as he and Bronco finished up. "I watched the two of you grow up, for fuck's sake—from little seedlings, into what you are today. You may not have been my own, but you might as well have been. Just promise me you'll keep li'l Gill safe, okay?"

Havoc nodded in confirmation, a silent declaration to the old man that no harm would come to Gillette during their trip.

The world stood still as Havoc took one final panoramic swoop of the city known as Paradise. Pensive apprehension consumed him. He considered the notion of never coming back a possibility. What if the promise of the West held his and Gillette's interest? What would become of their roots tying them to the desert landscape of Nevada? While not a place he would have lived in by choice, it worried him: the thought of Paradise becoming more a lost concept than an actual city (a place where all his past memories would rest, waiting for him to return) with every mile that disappeared beneath their feet.

"Are we almost ready to leave?" Gillette asked, a small tower of novels in her hands. "The day isn't getting any younger, and we both know the horrors that roam the streets at night."

"What's with all the books," Havoc said, perplexed. "I don't recall you *ever* reading a book before."

"True," Gillette placed the stack of literature on the floor of the backseat, "but I figured you could read me to sleep. I won't be able to watch movies like I normally would, so you reading to me will have to do during our trip."

"And you think we're going to need," Havoc counted, "eight novels throughout? That feels like overkill, if you ask me."

"Knowing how I am when it comes to reading, I'll probably get bored of every single one before you're even halfway through with them," Gillette giggled. "But I figured it could be a way for us to relive a childhood memory, of you reading to me whenever there was a power outage in the theater and my dad couldn't fix it before sundown. I always found it soothing, to hear you read aloud by candlelight as I drifted off."

Havoc said nothing. He blinked in disbelief.

"Just humor me, okay?"


A SIZABLE CROWD HAD GATHERED around the car, curious to see the two off. While the townspeople weren't strangers to the occasional passerby, coming and going before the day's end, they had never witnessed a native resident leave the hallowed grounds of Paradise. The older faces in the crowd wore varied looks of concern while children whispered their desire to join them, to feed their unchecked curiosities—see what shapeless wonders might rest beyond their home stretch of road and desert sand.

"Any idea when we should expect the two of you back from your little trip out west?" Ford asked as he slammed the trunk closed.

"We shouldn't be too long," Havoc said, his gaze lost to the enigmatic charm of whatever mysteries lie dormant on the other end of the horizon. "If we leave now, we should be at our destination before sundown; and we'll probably stay a day or two before heading back." He turned to face the old man with a smile. "So don't you worry, we'll be back before anyone is given the chance to miss us too much."

"And don't go doing any of your usual theatrics on the road," Ford chastised preemptively. "Just because I fitted you with brand new tires don't mean you can go crazy with them."

"Enough with the chitchat, you two," Gillette interrupted, eager and excited to head out. "If we're only going to be in L.A. for a couple of days, I would like to leave now if we can, please."

Without another exchange of words, Havoc and Gillette got into the car and waved goodbye to everyone who came to see them leave as the vehicle carried them away from the main road—away from any trace of familiarity, and into the void of the unknown.

A bittersweet energy filled the air. Because while the old city of Paradise slowly became nothing more than a fading image in the rearview mirror, Havoc couldn't help but feel a pained sadness in his chest. He couldn't explain it, but it refused to let up—even after the backdrop of the town's rather quaint simplicity disappeared into a cloud of dust.

*There's no place like home,* his mind whispered as the fair-weathered call of the Pacific coastline continued to pull him toward the edge of Nevada's lifeless horizon. But the further they drove—with the outline of Paradise no longer in sight, the town's existence now buried in the sand—the weight of its sentiment diminished. And by the time they reached the Interstate, their point of no return, the old familiar phrase had lost itself to a passing wind.

# CHAPTER 2

## ALL OF THE NEGATIVES

# §1

## WEST COAST AMBITIONS

AVOC STILL COULDN'T BELIEVE, after what felt like a lifetime living in Paradise—even with several miles now behind him—that he was back on the road, heading west toward the unknown. He had Gillette to thank for it. Had it not been for her insistence on watching a third film (to cleanse her mental palette of gun violence), he wouldn't have stayed the night with her and talked about leaving home for the Californian coastline; having her along during the journey was an added bonus.

With more than half his life spent tucked away from the call of the Interstate, his memory of an ever-changing horizon had nearly been forgotten. But after having rekindled his exposure to the world's majestic unfurling of an uncharted landscape, he marveled at the first sight of the Sierra Nevada off to the north—their jagged peaks forever reaching toward the heavens. They reminded him of home, waking up to the distant view of the Spring Mountains. A small voice whispered for him to turn back, but he ignored it; nothing, no amount of reconsideration, could convince him to abandon the idea of continuing onward.

He turned to find Gillette staring out the window, admiring what little scenery there was as it passed. A faint smile could be seen at the corner of her cheeks, and Havoc couldn't help but grin at the thought of enjoying such a simple pleasure.

"I never would have imagined California to share a similar terrain to Nevada," Gillette said as they passed the state border. "As a child I always pictured planted wheat fields and untamed hillsides. I never expected to leave the desolation of the Nevadan desert to find myself greeted by the same sand-filled roadside. It's a bit of a disappointment, if I'm being honest."

"Did you think the view would change the moment we crossed the state line?" Havoc laughed, finding Gillette's naivete rather amusing. "It might be a while before we leave the world of cacti and tumbleweeds behind, but we'll get there. You just have to give it time." He instinctively looked down at the center console, at the expressionless face of its digital clock—unable to recall the last time it functioned as such. "And by the look of things, we have all the time in the world."

"As long as you remember to find a place for us to sleep before sundown," his traveling companion commented. "I guess I can give California a second chance to impress me."

"You mean you don't want to sleep in the car?"

Gillette turned her attention away from the view outside her window to eye her friend with playful contempt, pretending to be unamused by his remark. "If that was supposed to be your attempt at making a joke, I'm not laughing." But she couldn't finish her insult without smiling.

"Don't lie. You thought it was funny."

"Not even crickets would've dignified it with a response."

"Your smile betrays you, you know."

"Just shut up and keep driving," Gillette said. Her attention returned to the barren canvas that was the Mojave Desert. "I'd hate to have to punch you while you're driving and risk us swerving off the main road."

"Stranded in the desert," Havoc replied. "What a pleasant way to spend the afternoon."

Gillette's eyes grew heavy as she watched the endless sea of sand pass beneath their feet. While the transition from Nevada to California had been anticlimactic, she still dreamed of the undeniable beauty of Los Angeles that lay just within reach. If anything resembling magic still existed, it would be in the city where so many tales of love, tragedy, and horror were immortalized on display for thousands to see around the world in the comfort of a darkened room on the silver screen; a celluloid dream for the masses.

"Wake me when the scenery *actually* becomes interesting." And with her eyes now closed, Gillette fell asleep to the humming lullaby of the car's engine, trusting Havoc at the wheel.


IT ALL HAPPENED SUDDENLY, with no time to react. The undisturbed silence of driving down the highway ended abruptly with a deafening pop, followed by a harsh shift in gravity. Havoc felt the car skid and pull in the opposite direction of the noise. And before he could assess the situation, the vehicle flipped. Everything in the backseat thrashed about, several cans of food and peanut oil having made their way to the front and slamming into the windshield before they bounced back to the other end of the vehicle, leaving their mark in the shape of cracks in the windshield's integrity. All he could manage to do during the chaos was send out a resigned prayer into the void for his and Gillette's safety as the car slowed to a complete halt.

Unaware to what transpired, Gillette opened her eyes to their current state of affairs. Still in a daze, she scanned the full interior of the cabin, laughing to herself at the mess of canned goods and books that now rest scattered along the ceiling.

"Who taught you how to drive?" she asked, still laughing.

# §2

## THE MOJAVE

ITH THE CAR RENDERED UNDRIVABLE, the two continued their journey west on foot, carrying what they could
manage—forced to leave a substantial amount of food
and other supplies behind until they found shelter for the evening and
could come back to collect the rest. And with the sun now in its slow
afternoon descent, they both knew they would have to find someplace
soon before nightfall; the horror stories they were told growing up reason enough to not want to be caught out in the open after sundown.

But no matter which way they went, nothing—not even an abandoned Sure Stop gas station—could be seen close enough to the main
road for refuge. Only the remnants of a small town rested several miles
away from the beaten path, in the opposite direction, adjacent to the
site of the wreckage. And having remembered Ford's countless stories

from his childhood, of ghost towns too far from the highway (and the many travelers lost to whatever haunts lived within them), Havoc didn't want to risk leaving the safety of the paved roadway for an evening's rest; even with the six shooter Ford had given him for protection loaded and resting against his thigh in its leather holster, and thirty-eight of the box's fifty .38 rounds skillfully placed around his waist.

"So much for getting us there by the end of the day," Gillette said, hoping to lighten the mood. "But at least now we'll have more time to ourselves along the way. And once we get there we can scream at the top of our lungs into the heart of the city, that way everyone in the world will know of our achievement."

"That's if we make it there at all," Havoc replied.

A hushed moment carried itself onto the scene. While an uncomfortable addition to the situation at hand, Havoc took advantage of the silence. With it safe to presume the rest of the trip would be made on foot, an inventory played out in his head. Ford and Bronco had packed enough food for them to last them four days—an overabundance had it all gone according to plan. But fate decided to deliver their good fortune elsewhere; any sense of certainty, gone. And should their current predicament remain a constant, with no opportunity to replenish their supplies, they would have to cut back if their provisions were to last from point A to point B and back again.

Havoc's thoughts of keeping inventory eventually lost themselves to the subtle rhythm of his and Gillette's footsteps; every combined measure conveyed an inescapable feeling of aimlessness the further they traveled from the wreckage. His curiosity never strayed far from the ghost town. He stopped for a moment to study his shadow, determining how long they would have before the earth surrendered itself to the twilight's ascendance of the moon.

Necessity outweighed unproven suspicion.

EXHAUSTION GREETED THEM when they arrived at the edge of the town's city limits, any desire for exploration dead upon arrival; a safe place to sleep their only concern. And as the sun disappeared behind the curtain of desert mountains, nary a word found itself uttered between the two as they hurried toward the nearest structure.

"Kind of reminds you of home, doesn't it?" Gillette said as they settled themselves in for the night.

"In the dark, everything feels familiar."

"We should explore the town a bit after sunrise, see if any hidden treasures lurk within."

Havoc nodded in response, considering the notion.

"Do you think everything in the car will be okay until morning?"

"It should be," Havoc said as he maneuvered through the building's blackened interior. "People hardly travel this time of year. The car could probably sit there until the summer months before anyone cared to stumble upon it."

"I still can't believe we actually left Paradise." Gillette's voice fell to the floor, finding comfort on the cold linoleum. "To think, just this morning we were back home; it feels like a dream. Wouldn't it be worth a laugh if we woke up still in the cineplex?"

"Considering the fact we no longer have a vehicle to get us to the coastline and back home," Havoc said, joining her on the ground. "I wouldn't mind waking up to find this had all been a nightmare."

Gillette sighed. "And as always, you fail to see the silver lining. Sure, we've been delayed by a few days—and yes, traveling on foot will prove itself tiresome—but now we can truly appreciate how far we've come from day-to-day. Instead, you would rather escape our current situation simply because you find the circumstances less than favorable to your liking." She paused. A breath of disappointment filled the air. "I guess some things never change."

Havoc sat in silence, unable to respond to Gillette's final statement. She always knew what to say to leave him speechless and feeling guilty for what he said. It helped he couldn't see her facial expression, though he knew it well: the look of discontent. He had grown up with it and could still sense its presence in the dark; seeing it would have crushed him completely.

"Why do we always do this?" he asked.

"What do you mean?"

"This." He gestured in vain. "We always end up arguing over some minor discrepancy. I expressed my feelings toward today's misfortune and you felt compelled to vaguely call attention to past conversations where we fell into an argument, however brief. And it's not just recently, either; we've always been this way, even as kids."

Another quiet episode befell them, yet another unfortunate part of their lifelong routine; the direction of the exchange an uncertainty until one of them broke the silence. And the death to their shared diffidence often came at the expense of the other's ego.

"It doesn't always have to be this way," Gillette said, her voice nearing a whisper.

"That's true, I guess."

"Old habits die hard," she continued, her words now barely audible as the promise of a good night's rest slowly carried her off. "But it's not like an effort can't be made to improve our . . . behavior—to try and avoid moments like this in the future. But it would require *both* of us to put forth a little work if we ever want to find a balance and reach a more desirable outcome—one where we're not constantly at each other's throats."

"A desire to communicate," Havoc whispered to himself, knowing their discussion had come to a close for the night—the subtle shift in Gillette's breathing a clear sign she had retired for the evening, leaving him alone with his thoughts. "If only it were that easy."

Beyond the sheltered safety of their makeshift hostel, the sound of the desert's nightlife could be heard in the distance scavenging the twilit landscape. He seized the grip of the revolver. While he had never held a firearm before earlier today—and he prayed he would never have to pull the trigger—the feel of cold wood and steel in the palm of his hand helped calm his nerves. But unlike his companion, the notion of sleep eluded him. A minor detail about today's blowout confused him. *If Ford had replaced the tires the day before we left, why did one of them pop unexpectedly?*

# §3

## FLAPJACKS & PHOTOGRAPHS

AGER TO COLLECT THE REST of their supplies from the wreck, having been unable to find rest throughout the night, Havoc set out for the Interstate before sunrise to salvage as much as he could before Gillette woke up and surprise her with breakfast.

He enjoyed the early morning, before daylight returned to the earth—to sit and watch as the void of midnight relinquished itself to a rich color palette of faded honey blossom, warm peach skin, and calla lily at an undemanding pace. To this day, he considered it a marvel to witness the sun's ability to breathe new life onto an otherwise lifeless planet. And while others would claim the same splash of brilliance occurred at sunset, he preferred its eastern counterpart.

Confusion met him when he arrived at the highway. Where the wreckage once rested, only fragments of shredded rubber remained.

Its sudden disappearance a mystery, he scanned the area for clues to how it could have been removed from the main road, but only a sand ridden terrain of cacti and street signs filled his view. The thought of returning empty handed troubled him; with the rest of the food and water gone, they would only last another day of travel before being forced to go without any form of nourishment. Doubt and dread consumed him. He didn't want to tell Gillette the unfortunate news — that they would have to turn back — but he promised Ford to keep her safe and he daren't test fate any further. Their only saving grace: if the ghost town they stayed the night in happened to have any canned goods to scavenge for themselves.

All he could do was pray and hope.


WHEN HE ARRIVED BACK IN TOWN, what Havoc saw in the light of day shook him to the bone. The place resembled a graveyard comprised of stripped down automobiles; skeletons of man-made machinery littered the area like a battlefield. The thought of someone dismantling a vehicle, robbing it of its identity, horrified him. Why would someone do such a thing? But among them, near the town's center, a tow truck sat parked outside an old schoolhouse; and on its bed rested his father's car, waiting to be unloaded and gutted like the rest of them.

Determined to save the vehicle from a similar fate, Havoc forged his way through the labyrinth of steel corpses. It bothered him to see the only reminder he had left of his father in such a way; its current condition a travesty to his memory. Not a moment existed in his lifetime where the car wasn't present. Even before he and his father left the warm security of eastern Nebraska, the car had always been a constant. Distant memories of cruising around town replayed in his head as he ran his hand across the vehicle's metal frame — of driving to the other side of town, circling the grain tower twice before they stopped at the edge of the field where his parents worked from sunrise until the early hours of the afternoon while he climbed every nearby tree and dreamed of adventure.

He had pictured it differently, that the car would have lived on to see another generation of travel, and finally finish what he and his father started when he was younger. But that would all die here, in an unnamed town in the middle of nowhere among an endless field of disassembled, weather-worn brethren.

"Can I help you with something?" a man's voice asked.

Havoc turned to find an armored individual pointing a rifle at him. He raised his hands instinctively, to prove he wasn't a threat. And going by the stranger's shaky demeanor, neither was he. Unlike the cowboys from old Westerns, his aim lacked confidence; the barrel trembled in small circles of uncertainty. The only advantage the squatter had on him was makeshift body armor: an awkward arrangement of dismantled car parts.

"I'll ask you again." The man's grip tightened on the weapon. "Can I help you with something?"

"Do you mind lowering your firearm first?"

The man's gaze shifted to Havoc's holster. Havoc could see every far-fetched scenario playing itself out in the stranger's eyes, weighing each outcome mathematically in order to determine the best course of action. He asked if the revolver was loaded, and Havoc nodded silently in response. More calculations sped through the man's facial cues before he finally lowered the rifle.

"Last chance before this has to get ugly," he said, still sounding nervous. "Can I help you with something?"

"If it's not too much trouble, I would like to retrieve whatever valuables are left in my vehicle that you've somehow managed to tow from the street. A friend and I were just passing through and—"

"Oh, you must be who Gillette was talking about," the man interrupted. He moved toward Havoc, his right arm outstretched. "We were just talking about you and your guys' situation over breakfast.

Please forgive me for the rude introduction." He looked down at his firearm, feeling embarrassed. "One can never be too careful out here in the desert. The name's Macro, by the way. Now please, let's head inside. I'll fix you something to eat."

Havoc followed Macro into the schoolhouse, leaving the cemetery behind. He laughed at each step his guide made, the sound of metal on metal echoing through the halls whenever one piece clashed with another—curious to know how he managed to sneak up on him outside without alerting him to his presence.

The building's interior had a haunting quality surrounding it; beyond the main lobby, with its empty hallways lined with steel lockers and barred windows that stretched toward the ceiling, everything left Havoc feeling claustrophobic. How anyone could call this place home puzzled him.

As they continued down the main hallway Macro mentioned how the place used to be full of life—how you couldn't walk down a single corridor without bumping elbows with someone else, the air filled to the ceiling with a cacophonous breath of conversation—until one day he woke to find everyone else had left unannounced without him, leaving the town all to himself . . . always wondering if anyone would ever come back. But as Macro carried on with his own run of misfortune while they dove deeper into the belly of the school, Havoc's attention drifted toward the walls. A collage of printed photographs lined the interior the further they went; scattered at first, but eventually becoming a disorganized mess. He glossed over the details the longer he stared at the wall, afraid if he lingered on one image for too long he would lose himself to its hypnotic spell.

"It's a great way to pass the time," Macro said as he led them both downstairs to the cafeteria, having noticed Havoc's sudden fixation. "It really forces you to slow down and focus. You learn to pause and truly appreciate the beauty of a moment within a moment, to become one with time. And at the end of it, after the moment has passed, you can always look back—remember fondly how you waited for the perfect snapshot, and *click!* it's yours forever. What better way is there to own the end of the world?"

"If only for a second," Havoc sighed, exhausted by such a visual overload.

Macro turned and smiled at Havoc's comment. The expression appeared wounded, as if it were the first time in a while since he last done so without forcing it—almost a foreign notion.

"About time you got back," Gillette said as the two entered the cafeteria, still eating from her plate. "I was beginning to think *both* of you decided to just leave me here." She glared at Havoc as she took a bite from her fork.

"I found him out front eyeing the car on the bed of my truck."

"Macro was kind enough to remove it from the highway. Now please, don't just stand there—join me. Our host made . . . what are they called again?"

"Flapjacks."

"Yes, those! They're delicious."

"Thank you, but I think I'll pass," Havoc said as he sat next her. "I just wanted to collect the rest of our belongings and have a quick meal before heading back on the road."

"Don't insult the man," Gillette whispered. "We're guests in his home, after all."

Havoc turned to Macro in an air of defeat. "I guess I'll have a few."

"Great! I'll go cook some more up!" Macro jumped from his seat delighted. "They're an old family recipe my mother used to whip up before . . . well, before everyone left."

Havoc watched as the *lord of the manor* headed for the kitchen and removed his armor to fix both of them a short stack. Underneath the metal plating, a surprisingly built individual existed; a stark contrast to his frail temperament.

"So what took you two so long?"

"We got held up having a three-way staring contest between him, myself, and his rifle."

"It's not loaded," she said through a mouthful. "Told me he only fired it twice and didn't care for the aftermath it caused."

"And what was that?"

"Killed a drifter and his son."

"Was it self defense?"

"Yes, but I'm sure that didn't lessen the effect it had on his soul. The father died instantly—head shot—but the boy didn't die until a couple of days later due to infection. Told me he tried to save him, but the bullet had splintered off into smaller pieces on impact; he couldn't find every fragment."

"Christ. . . . How long ago? Did he say?"

"It was—"

"And here we are! Two short stacks and an extra helping for the young lady, should she still be hungry." Macro winked and sat on the other end of the booth, proud of his culinary creation. "Gillette here told me you two are heading toward the coast. Sounds exciting. What draws you out that way?"

"I made a promise to myself to finish what my father and I started when I was younger and Gillette has always had an affinity for the magic of cinema."

"Cinema?" Macro said, confused.

"Sorry. When Havoc says cinema, he means motion pictures."

Macro shook his head and shrugged while he positioned his fork and knife to prepare his first bite."

"Does this town not have a movie theater?"

Again, Macro shook his head.

Gillette turned to Havoc, her eyes wide with disbelief. It never occurred to her that anyone could've lived their entire life without the gift of watching the miracle of Hollywood bleed from the silver screen as she did growing up. She sat back for a moment, still trying to comprehend the difference between Macro's and her upbringing; her appetite lost to such a realization.

AFTER BREAKFAST MACRO offered a tour of his home. It had become clear to them both that he missed socializing with others and wanted them to stay a while longer, a gracious host desperate for company who only wanted to continue heading west toward the Pacific.

"While I may not have had the privilege of having a movie theater in town, the schoolhouse was blessed with a reference center." He motioned his guests through the open door. "Growing up, before I found photography, this place was my sanctuary. One could lose an entire day here, their mind elsewhere while lost in the pages of someone else's imagination."

"Look at you two," Gillette said as she scoped the library's titles row by row. "Cut from the same cloth."

"I noticed a small collection of books in the back seat of your car when I towed it. From the design of some of their covers, none of them looked familiar, and it's been a while since I've had the chance to read something new."

"You're welcome to take some of them off our hands." Havoc eyed Gillette from across the room. "*Someone* brought one too many."

"Nonsense," laughed Macro. "When it comes to the world of literature, there's no such thing as *too many*."

They continued in silence for a spell. Havoc and Gillette drifted through every aisle, surprised to find an unfamiliar title from time to time. And whenever they crossed paths, Havoc smirked when he caught a glimpse of her mouthing the names of authors. While they had shared many an afternoon in a darkened auditorium, the experience of watching Gillette study the spines of such literary artifacts felt intimate: the motion of her eyes as they scrutinized every letter—a small spark of curiosity made apparent when she reached out to remove the novel from the shelf so she could read the brief synopsis on the back. It reminded him of when they were children, discovering themselves through the art of cinema; their likes and dislikes.

"You know," Macro's voice hovered in the air. "If you two find anything you haven't already read, and you're open to parting with some of the books in your car, I'd be open to making a trade."

The two exchanged glances but didn't speak a word; they didn't have to. Havoc knew Gillette would be open to the idea—giving Macro something new to read for the first time in years—and Gillette knew Havoc would decline the notion of an even exchange; instead, opting to simply give him the books he wanted without transaction. If they were to make the rest of the trip on foot, they would need to sacrifice any unnecessary weight, and eight books would prove more a hindrance than anything. But Gillette would counter his offer by holding up the novel in her hands. Havoc nodded but followed it with a wide-eyed stare, letting her know it would be their only compromise.

"You two still there?"

"Tell you what," Havoc said, breaking the silence. "You can take the ones you said looked new to you and all it'll cost you is one book from your home library."

Gillette bit her lower lip as she smiled. Havoc returned the gesture with a grin of his own. He could read the excitement in her eyes. It was the same look she used to make when they were younger, when he would read to her after lights out and she couldn't sleep—which was more often than not after the raid. But the look in her eyes carried a different weight to it now than it did in the past. A brightness filled her gaze; it felt familiar to the subtle glow of their candlelit evenings as adolescents, when they could fill the void with aimless conversation and thought they had all the time in the world.

Although he would never admit it to Gillette, if anything worthwhile were to come from their trip to Los Angeles, he would consider the revival of a late-night childhood ritual one of them.

# §4

## EFFORTLESS SYMMETRY

THEY CONTINUED THEIR TOUR upstairs on the second floor. Excited to show his guests his darkroom, Macro walked with a skip in his step. Gillette playfully matched his energy, but Havoc couldn't help but notice the position of the sun outside whenever they passed a window. And if the pace of their guided tour continued at its already sedated speed, travel would have to wait another day. But he couldn't bring himself to mention his desired haste to leave the further Macro led them into the building, and it didn't take long for morbid curiosity to suppress his hunger for the open road.

*Los Angeles will always be there to welcome us when we arrive.*

A feeling of déjà vu overwhelmed him when they reached their destination. All along the doorway lived a mess of photographed imagery, most of them quaint in their execution: still framed snapshots of seemingly random locations Macro considered inspiring, their central focus a street sign or passing tumbleweed; the rest of the image lost in a blur. Others painted a rather grim reality—a small window into his world of isolation. Havoc couldn't even begin to fathom the extent of the man's loneliness. Even during his self-imposed solitude on the outskirts of Paradise, he always had the option to drive fifteen minutes into town and feed the occasional desire to socialize with others. The thought of it no longer a possibility terrified him.

"I know you said it's a great way to pass the time," Havoc said as he continued to scan the arch of the doorway, "but I'm curious to hear what initially sparked your interest."

Gillette nudged him with an elbow.

"An unfortunate incident, I'm afraid," Macro answered. He opened the door and stepped to the side, waving his guests to enter before him. "But beauty has a funny way of following shortly after a tragedy."

An unexplained hesitation held Havoc and Gillette in place. Past the room's threshold they both sensed a somber mood lurking somewhere in the shadows—its icy cold fingers reaching for them in vain; a captive to its own desperate environment—but Macro's welcoming posture dictated they carry through with the invitation, and sympathy soon overruled their reservations.

Once inside, with the door closed behind them, a second passed in total darkness before the room saw itself illuminated by a solitary red light bulb; its crimson hue imparting an already tightly knit living space with a sinister atmosphere. And like the archway outside, not an inch of wall-space had been left untouched by the printed outline of an already developed photograph.

"Whenever I find myself beginning to slip into an episode of non-existence, I'll lock myself in here for a day or two and sort through all of the negatives—experiment with color gradients and symmetry, just for fun." Macro took a step back and admired every creation of his as they stared back at him. "It's cathartic — to watch an image come to life, and to be the one to do it: something from the past immortalized for anyone to see well into the future once I'm gone, should they happen to stumble upon it."

"Color gradients and symmetry?"

"Image manipulation," Macro said. He pulled three prints down from the wall and handed them to his guest. "By altering the contrast of the photograph — by eliminating or creating shadow, and countless other forms of modification — you can shape the narrative to whatever you wish to convey to the viewer. An empty hallway can either come across as hopeless and devoid of history or the complete opposite: full of promise, with a story to tell."

"Fascinating," Gillette said as she studied the once two identical images over Havoc's shoulder. "How so much can be said with very little." Her attention shifted to the third example: a mirrored black and white panoramic of one of the school's many hallways. It appeared seamless, the only indication of its artificial nature being a duplicate of a tree with a knot on one of its leafless branches. But only a critical eye would have known to catch the abnormality.

"It's another reason why I've developed such a fondness for the craft in more recent years." Macro continued along the perimeter of the room, looking for other examples. "Unlike the novel's rigid temperament — whose well-established narrative never varies, even with subsequent readings; consistent to a fault — a single photograph can communicate an endless road of possibility, each one entirely reliant on both the picture's composition and the observer's interpretation of the image at hand."

Havoc cleared his throat with derision.

"What is it?"

"I'd argue that its subjective nature would only dampen the weight of its impact," Havoc said. He examined both variations one last time before he returned each photo to their rightful place on the wall and shook his head, annoyed by Macro's point of view.

"What do you mean?" Macro asked.

"A novel, a work of literature, is *written and designed* to illicit an emotional or cerebral response from its audience." Havoc grabbed the book from Gillette's hand and flipped through its pages from cover to cover. "There's a clear story being told here, from beginning to end. Sure, the narrative remains constant, but its impact—much like that of a photograph—can vary depending on the reader."

"I don't think he meant to—"

"And any breath of influence carried forth by an unmoving image only exists for the individual dissecting it," Havoc continued over Gillette's attempt to diffuse the situation. "But therein lies the only beauty of its existence: it can mold its significance to whatever the percipient needs it to be . . . *for them.* Other than that, it's a spiritless recreation of a moment in time no longer present. It may mean something to you, being the one who took the snapshot, but I look at all these prints on the wall and feel nothing. Meanwhile, a novel can mean something to someone else *other than its creator.*"

"Havoc."

"What?"

"I really don't think he meant anything by it."

"If what I said insulted you in any way, I apologize," Macro said. "I didn't mean to denounce the generalized impact of literature, simply that the medium of photography has, at the moment, taken its place in my life. And who knows, perhaps the paradigm will shift again and land me somewhere else in the near future. Perhaps I'll venture beyond the boundaries of my hometown one day, much like you two did, and find a place where motion pictures exist and fall in love with what you two have referred to as *cinema.*"

Gillette told him about Paradise—how she and Havoc had grown up on a variety of films throughout their childhood—and if he should ever go through with the idea of leaving town, to head northeast along the highway until he saw the giant Ferris wheel. If she and Havoc weren't going to be there to enjoy a noonday matinee, she would want someone to do so in their stead; help keep the tradition alive until they got back from their trip.

Moved by Gillette's sentiment, Macro ambled toward one of his work stations and opened a small drawer on a steel cabinet. He sorted through a mess of old folders and paper until he managed to find and retrieve something compact and rectangular from its depths, along with a couple of small, cardboard packages. "I realize the day is almost over and you'll have to wait until tomorrow to leave," he said, handing them all three items. "But please, take this as a token of my appreciation for spending the day with me. It's been years since I've had someone to converse with—and for that, I'm grateful."

"What are they?" Gillette asked.

"A Polaroid camera and two pockets of film."

"I'm not sure that answers her question."

"Instant photography," Macro said as he demonstrated. "First, you load your film through the bottom, just below the shutter. After that, all you have to do is point and click; the picture ejects from here, and within ten to fifteen minutes you'll have an image to remember from your trip. And you never know what might catch your eye."

Havoc weighed the device in his hands. He considered its general design straightforward and easy to use, but he couldn't imagine a scenario where he would want to keep a permanent record of a point in time on film. "I'm sorry," he said with apprehension, "but I don't know if we can accept this."

"Please. I know it may not appear like much, but once you've taken your first snapshot you'll find yourself wanting to capture every moment you come across. Here, I'll show you." Macro took the camera back and motioned everyone back into the hallway.

Havoc and Gillette watched as he measured the lighting of their surroundings. It only took him a second before he repositioned them against a wall facing the sun, rearranged their arms in a cordial embrace and told them to smile. The process of posing for a photograph felt pedestrian (forced to remain as motionless as possible while they waited for Macro to follow through with the simple task of pressing a button—being asked to move to either the left or right until they found the *perfect spot*), but Havoc appreciated the atmosphere of intimacy he currently shared with Gillette; its artificial nature didn't bother him. And at the end of it, a pocket-sized reminder he knew he would cherish forever.

THEIR TOUR ENDED OUTSIDE among the skeletal remains of automobiles at sunset. Havoc didn't care for the reintroduction, an unfriendly admonition that his father's car would soon find itself among them. It truly bothered him, to know its lifespan would end with him and the opportunity to live on for another generation or two traveling the roads of the Wasteland now remained a nostalgic daydream.

"I still can't believe you did *all of this* by yourself," Gillette said, still astonished by the volume of disassembled chassis that littered the town. "How long did it take you to dismantle each vehicle to its bare components?"

"About two to three days, depending on the make and model."

"But why?" Havoc asked.

"Why?"

"Yes, why," he continued. "Why would anyone want to strip a vehicle of everything that made it what it was meant to be? I mean . . . it's apparent you used some of the scrap metal for your body armor, but what ever became of the engine? The axle? All the other major components that helped bring it to life. What happened to them?"

Macro pointed to a tall building on the other side of town. "They found a home at the old steel mill."

"Were all these vehicles here to begin with?" He scanned the area and counted nineteen metal skeletons in his field of view alone.

"Not all of them, no," Macro laughed. "Only the first six were left behind when I woke up alone in town. Most of them I've managed to collect over a period of time; some came in high frequency, others few and far between. But after my little       run-in a few years back, given their motivations, I decided it would be to my benefit if I stripped them of any functional appeal. And while it can get lonesome out here in the desert, I'd happily live the rest of my days alone than risk attracting the *wrong kind of attention* again and again." He paused to watch the final ridge of the evening sun fall behind the mountains on the horizon. "And with that, we should head in and call it a night. As I'm sure you're well aware, wild catamounts are nocturnal and will be hunting for food to bring back to their young. And I think I can speak for everyone when I say I'd rather we stay off the menu tonight."


BACK IN THE SAFE, SUBTERRANEAN DEPTHS of the cafeteria, Havoc watched as Macro and Gillette slept peacefully under the subdued lighting overhead. His mind wandered elsewhere, to the days and miles ahead of them. He knew the road to Los Angeles wouldn't be easy on foot, but he convinced himself the trip would prove itself worth the trouble—a conscious effort to stray from his usual line of cynicism on Gillette's behalf.

His fading gaze shifted to his lap, where the printed image of him and Gillette rested. He smiled at the thought of taking her picture the moment they arrived at their destination, to capture her genuine reaction on film when she finally set foot in her favorite place on earth.

# CHAPTER 3
## KEEP IT LIKE A SECRET

# §1

## LIFE BEFORE PARADISE

"ARE YOU SURE you two can't stay another day?" Macro asked as Havoc and Gillette loaded the last of their supplies into a shopping cart they found outside an old, abandoned mini-mart. "It's just . . . I've come to enjoy having someone to talk to again, you know? And it felt nice to not feel completely alone for a change."

"We'll see each other again," Gillette said, hoping to ease the pain of saying goodbye. "Your place is on the way back home, after all. You can always keep yourself occupied with your photography until we find our way back here. And there's always Paradise if you get lonely."

"And let's not forget you have a whole new stack of books to enjoy once we leave," Havoc chimed in. "That should distract you from the thought of our absence for a spell."

"We'll see." Macro forced a smile. "I guess we'll see."

A silence developed between the three of them. It felt bittersweet, to acknowledge the inevitability of their departure. Empty promises to cross paths in the future would keep their spirits high for a few weeks before reality eventually revealed them as another fruitless sentiment, the passing of time their only certainty. And as they parted ways, the faint sound of Macro's camera could be heard in the background: a last ditch effort on his part to keep them with him once their silhouettes disappeared into the skyline.

"Do you think he'll be okay?" Gillette asked.

"He's lasted this long all by himself, hasn't he? I think he'll be all right without us. And it's like you said, he can always head to Paradise if he gets lonely."

TRAVELING THROUGH THE HUSHED MONOCHROME of the California desert allowed Havoc's thoughts to roam. Having spent most of his life surrounded by sand, he learned to appreciate its empty and desolate disposition. While he remembered bits and pieces from his childhood before he and his father left the green grass fields of Nebraska, he preferred Nevada's arid consistency; whatever lived in the desert survived well enough on its own, no upkeep required. And nothing lie buried underneath its surface, threatening destruction. Deep down, he prayed California's landscape remained the same all the way to the Pacific coastline, with no secret oasis awaiting their arrival.

"How far do you think we'll get today?" Gillette asked.

"While Macro and I sorted through the stack of books left in the car he told me the next town is about sixty-four miles away. But if we keep a steady pace, we should be there just after nightfall."

"Um, excuse me. Did you say *after nightfall?*"

Havoc nodded, confirming his previous statement. He watched Gillette's eyes widen. A shapeless terror stopped her dead in her tracks. She went to protest, but fear held her tongue. All Havoc could do was urge her to continue onward, that any delay in their travels would only put them more at risk of being caught in the middle of nowhere after sundown.

HE CURSED A FAMILY OF CLOUDS as they carried themselves overhead at high noon, consuming the world in a blanket of endless shadow. Without the sun to help him tell the time, he feared the worst. In a desperate attempt to not fall behind, he took control of the shopping cart, shoved the supplies to the front end, and convinced Gillette to sit among the cans and bottles of food and water. She understood the sudden rush; an overcast sky proved deadly with certain wildlife. And being in uncharted territory did little to comfort them, where they could only presume what unknown creatures lurked on the outskirts of the main road waiting for an opportunity to leave their underground habitats to scavenge the open Wasteland for anything they could consume.

Minutes passed before a break in the cloud cover flirted an unveiling of the sun. Gillette closed her eyes and stretched out her arms to welcome its warmth back to the earth while Havoc continued to push them forward at an alarming pace, enjoying the subtle breeze as it passed. It helped to quell whatever fear loomed in the corner of her mind, that they would make it to wherever they were heading before the final moments of the evening's afterglow faded into twilight.

She lowered her arms and took hold of the shopping cart, lost in a daydream. If only for a second, the world she knew faded into the background—its modest color palette replaced with one she grew up knowing intimately on the silver screen.

"Bring me the horizon," she whispered into the wind, looking forward to the future.

GILLETTE TOOK OVER for the final leg of the day's journey, despite Havoc's relentless protest. She worried about him, having refused a moment's rest for food or water. And every time she offered some of her beans or a sip from her bottle he would decline, saying he was neither hungry or thirsty, but she knew her friend well enough to know when he was lying. She watched as he counted every can in front of him; a silent obsession he brought with him from his childhood, when he and his father traveled halfway across the country—foraging for whatever they could find to survive along the way.

"Havoc?"

"Yeah?"

"Tell me about where you're from—the place you and your father called home before setting roots in Paradise. We've known each other most of our lives and you never really mentioned it until that night in the theater, when you talked about your mother and how she died."

"What's to tell?"

"Was it beautiful?" she asked. "Were there other families living on the land, or was it just the three of you? Did the town have a name? If so, what was it? Tell me everything. I'm curious. I want to know more about you, and what better place to start—if anywhere—than the small amount of time before you came into my life?"

Havoc repositioned himself to face Gillette while he spoke, to commit to the conversation. "Words could never do it justice, I'm afraid. Any attempt at capturing its beauty with the imagination would only prove itself a futile effort. It truly was a pretty little town."

"Try anyway," Gillette said with a smile. She watched as Havoc's tired gaze shifted to his left, attempting to recall the past as it rested in subdued secrecy somewhere on the peripheral edge of his memory. His pale blue eyes softened by several degrees, matching the sky in hue, while a faint smirk elevated the rest of his features deep into the stratosphere.

"I remember an endless sea of green. It didn't matter where you looked, life surrounded you. One could get lost in a mixed meadow of wildflowers during the summer season. And twenty minutes east of town, a river flowed. Mom would—" He paused, the words caught in his throat. His eyes had glazed over with a splash of melancholy. "She used to wash our clothes in the water and hang them to dry outside before she started on supper while father finished work in the fields."

"Sounds like something out of a dream," Gillette said.

"There are days where it feels that's all it was."

"Was it just the three of you?"

"No, there were other families living there. It was often pointed out by the older children that my parents were transplants, having moved there only a year before I was born. Nevertheless, we always felt welcome. And if it hadn't been for the explosion that consumed the town, we probably would have never left."

"As cruel as it may sound, I'm glad you and your father were forced to leave. Had it not been for that unfortunate incident, we would have never met each other. And while not ideal, we wouldn't be on our current journey to the Pacific coastline."

Havoc laughed. "You know something, Gill—while your sentiment may appear unconventional on the surface, and a bit insensitive to a certain degree, I find it hard to argue with its logic."

Gillette joined him in a warm fit of laughter. It felt good, to share a radiant moment, however fleeting. She looked ahead to find a distant outline of a town just off the main road. "It looks like we're about to arrive at our next stop."

"And with enough sunlight to explore a bit before turning in for the evening." Havoc turned to face Gillette with a mocking grin. "And you were worried."

"Shut up!"

Havoc kept quiet, knowing he risked a bruised shoulder if he continued any further.

"So," Gillette said, hoping to change the subject. "Did this perfect little town of yours have a name?"

"It did. The children always called it home; we had no use for anything else since we never left the compound. But the adults who traveled elsewhere for trade with nearby villages acknowledged it by the name found on a few buildings scattered throughout town from its previous lifetime, and they all called it Ithaca."

# §2

## ~~WELCOME TO~~ BARSTOW
### ~~STAY AWAY FROM~~

NOTHER OUTBREAK of achromatic cloud cover consumed what little sunlight lived in the sky, stripping the world of any semblance of color and leaving it in a blanket of lifeless gray. Disturbed by the sudden shift in atmosphere, Gillette scrambled toward the off ramp. With every hurried step she wondered how the town up ahead would welcome them; if the residents would greet them with open arms, or if they would stumble into another ghost town scenario, with a singular individual occupying its abandoned infrastructure—a collection of dismantled vehicles littering the area.

But as they inched their way into the city limits, a nameless dread dominated the senses. A wake of vultures crowded together, picking apart what remained of their evening meal. Havoc and Gillette looked on in discomposed horror every time their beaks rose from the earth with a mess of flesh and viscera. They both turned back to the main road, silently weighing the pros and cons of either staying in town until sunrise, or if they should risk the chance of running into other California wildlife along the Interstate during the night; the distant call and response of wild coyotes howling on the horizon convinced them to head deeper into their newfound surroundings. The town's conditions didn't improve the further they traveled. No matter which way they looked, death occupied the scene—most of the bodies already picked through and casually discarded, letting nature finish their decomposition. It all felt like a fever dream, where every step lent itself to yet another layer of panic-stricken suspense . . . and escape was not an option.

"What do you think happened here?" Gillette asked as they continued toward the town's center.

"My first guest would've been a drifter ambush," Havoc replied as he continued to scan the area. "But the details don't add up. Some of these bodies are women and children, and we both know they prefer to take them captive for . . . well, you know."

"Right."

"But whatever happened, it was recent."

They proceeded with caution as they marched forward, their target the town's main church building, a towering cathedral; its monolithic presence would have cast a shadow, had the overarching cloud cover not already thrown the world into a state of darkness. If anyone still lived in the city, their best bet for finding them would be the tallest structure—a guaranteed safe haven from anything that wished to cause them harm.

"It's so sad," Gillette said as they ambled down the road, stumbling across a new crop of corpses. "These people probably never saw it coming, whatever caused such a massacre to occur. And the weight of this town's demise would've probably gone unnoticed for a while longer, had we not experienced our little setback with the car. All this death . . . it would have remained a secret otherwise."

"Let's just pray it's not something contagious, or we'll be joining them soon enough."


WHEN THEY FINALLY ARRIVED at the church building it appeared less secure than it originally had from a distance: its windows had all been shattered, with wooden boards once used as benches and pews nailed haphazardly across every frame from the inside—preventing anyone from using them as a point of entry. They circled the perimeter looking for an opening, but the search proved itself a fruitless effort. All they managed to find was a note on the front door:

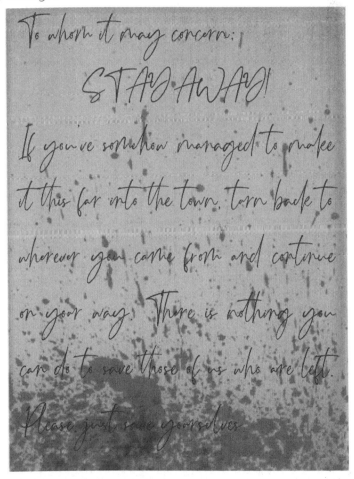

To whom it may concern:

STAY AWAY!

If you've somehow managed to make it this far into the town, turn back to wherever you came from and continue on your way. There is nothing you can do to save those of us who are left.

Please, just save yourselves.

"I wonder if anyone's still here," Gillette said.

"Whoever lives here, if they're even still alive, they obviously don't want anyone else getting in anytime soon."

"Still, I doubt it'll hurt to knock."

"The note clearly told us to turn back."

"It's nighttime! Jesus, Havoc, you can't be serious. Our chances of survival out on the road would be next to none compared to spending the night in a city-wide necropolis."

"Gill—"

"No! We've managed to come this far into town for shelter, to get away from the gruesome scenery all throughout this place, so I refuse to be turned away by a *fucking piece of paper*."

"Gill."

"What?"

Havoc said nothing, but his panic-eyed stare urged Gillette to turn around. She froze, unable to wrap her head around what was happening. An unspeakable sight emerged from the dirt in front of her very eyes; several of the corpses had lifted themselves from their dormant state, a soulless expression on their waxen faces. She turned her attention back to Havoc, who had yet to remove himself from a state of petrified terror—his skin now pale, his brow beaded by a cold, fear-stricken sweat.

"Gill."

"Yeah?"

"I'm going to need you to get down and cover your ears."

"Okay."

Everything slowed to a near-standstill, the consequence of every action amplified to its Nth degree. Havoc reached for the revolver as he counted the number of bodies now standing, preparing to take aim; five stood before him. Nervous, he released the cylinder from its frame and double-checked to make sure it was fully loaded. *The gunfight is in the head, not the hands*, he reminded himself as he snapped the cylinder back into place. He held his breath and cleared his head as he felt the weight of his thumb pull the hammer away from the firing pin. Seconds continued to pass in slow motion, but the first shot escaped the short length of the barrel before he could have any real influence to the bullet's trajectory.

The resounding echo of the gunshot breathed a cheerless sigh upon impact; his intended target only flinched at the shoulder for a brief moment but lost no momentum to its staggering stride. All five walking corpses let out an unimpressed moan as they continued to stumble their way toward the building. *Only five shots left, better make them count.*

Again, he cleared his mind and only focused on the threat ahead. But doubt now coursed through the nerves in his fingers, preventing him from pulling the trigger a second time. His hands shook, unable to steady them long enough to aim the firearm where he wanted the next shot to go.

*The gunfight is in the head, not the hands . . . The gunfight is in the head, not the hands . . . The gunfight is in the head, not the—*

BUT BEFORE HAVOC COULD CALM HIMSELF, the cathedral's doors swung open, hitting him with a small gust of wind. An older woman in blood-stained garments and a lab coat stormed past the threshold wielding a 12 gauge pump-action shotgun. He watched as she continued her way toward the undead gathering—her gait unwavering as the distance between her and her mark reduced itself to an arm's length. He couldn't bring himself to look away, not even when she leveled the barrel at the closest one's head and dispatched the first shot.

Not sparing a second, the woman maintained her sense of rhythm, continuing down the line; every motion she made marked with unmatched precision. Three more went down (now headless) before she changed her approach for the last one standing. Her grip moved to the weapon's now warm steel tubing; its stock high in the air. Without remorse, she swung for the head. But even after gravity claimed its final victim, the woman continued to swing until she felt satisfied with the results. A few minutes passed in the aftermath before she collected herself and started her way back to the church.

"Havoc? Is everything okay?" Gillette asked, her ears still covered and eyes shut tight.

Unable to speak, Havoc holstered his pistol and removed Gillette's hands from her ears and gently tapped her on the shoulder. Horrified by the violent development, Gillette retreated into Havoc's arms for safety. Their panicked hearts raced together in silent unison to their current situation, neither one of them able to comprehend the recent chain of events.

None of it felt real.

Havoc wished they had never left Paradise, and presumed Gillette would feel the same way after tonight.

The woman approached them still holding the shotgun by its barrel, her face without a discernible expression as she looked them both over, searching for injuries of any kind.

"If you're both able to walk on your own," she said as she finished examining them and stepped through the open doorway, "I'd make the wise decision of joining the woman who just saved you from becoming a late-night snack for a handful of shamblers. Don't take too long to decide, either; rumor has it she's been one to change her mind in a matter of seconds and will lock the door behind her without a second thought, leaving the two of you to die."

Without a moment's hesitation, they followed her inside.

# §3

---

# A HIDDEN UNDERWORLD

ILD RELIEF SET IN as Havoc and Gillette settled into their new surroundings, the interior of the cathedral's main hall far more welcoming than its outer appearance had originally implied; its construction an otherworldly marvel. Not a single angle of its composition lay to waste. Everything served a purpose.

"Forgive me if I don't turn on the lights," the woman said. She motioned toward one of the broken windows. "I found out the hard way that shamblers are attracted to artificial light, like moths to a flame."

"We're not strangers to living in the dark," Havoc replied.

A derisive smirk found the corner of the woman's lips. "So what brings a couple of tourists this far into Barstow?" she asked. "We've never been a town known for the occasional visit from a small group of random passersby, not even on a good day."

"We were just passing through," Gillette answered.

"Passing through?"

"I believe that's what she said."

"Nobody's ever *passed* through Barstow. Even before the town became what it is today, a living graveyard, nobody ever *passed* through here. We're a ghost town, in every sense of the word these days; God's dirty little secret. So I'll ask again: What brings you two this far into Barstow?"

Gillette bowed her head in wilted defeat, intimidated by the woman's commanding presence. "We just needed a place to sleep for the night."

The woman turned to deadbolt and chain the door, letting the answer sink in. "Which way are you heading?" she asked.

"Los Angeles."

The woman laughed. "You should've kept driving. The next town is only half an hour west from here. If you leave now you'll still have most of the night to catch some shut eye."

"We've been traveling on foot," Havoc told her. He watched the woman turn to him in disbelief. "And with the wilderness being what it is at nighttime, stopping here was our only option."

"Let's just hope we all make it to sunrise."

"What's that supposed to mean?" Havoc eyed the woman's firearm; she had yet to put it down.

"It means survival is no longer a certainty around here, and hasn't been for little over a month. I've watched this town devolve into what it is—bore witness to its downfall, no matter how hard I tried to prevent it from getting worse." The woman paused and turned away, her back now to her guests. She finally let the shotgun fall to the floor; her tired gaze followed shortly after. "All our hard work, along with everything we were hoping to achieve, and all it led to was *this*: a mountain of depravity and death."

"Havoc, she's scaring me," Gillette whispered.

"What *did* happen here, if you don't mind me asking?"

The woman's attention returned to the two of them, her eyes now red with grief as tears threatened to fall at any moment. "You would never understand."

"We have until morning, with nowhere to go until then," Havoc pointed out, persistent. "We've got time."

A collection of exhausted moans traveled through every broken window and into the main hall. Everyone's curiosity narrowed in on the front entrance, where an audience of the undead had gathered, desperate to get inside; their monosyllabic demands were soon followed by a series of abrupt collisions as they threw their bodies against their wooden obstruction. Paralyzed by reverent fear, Havoc watched as the swarm's efforts slowly started to produce results when the boards began to splinter.

"How much longer do you think this little barricade of yours will last?" he asked, half-afraid to hear the answer.

"If they keep going at it as hard as they are, not long enough," the woman answered as she knelt down to pick up her shotgun. "Quick, grab your cart of supplies and follow me to the back. Even if a horde of those things manage to get into the main hall, they won't be able to come after us once we're down in the lower levels. Now hurry—we might only have seconds."

The woman led them through the length of the sanctuary, past the stage and the altar, all the way to where the leading parish would have resided. The sound of fractured wood hitting the floor echoed through the building as she opened the door leading into the Father's living quarters. "Come on," she said, rushing her undesired guests into the room. "I'd prefer it if they didn't see where we ran off to."

The room rest threadbare and unassuming, stripped of personality. Only a throw rug and a bookshelf (with only a handful of books and a small family of framed photographs on display: their escort in one of them, embracing a child—a boy) occupied its small living space; the only reminder any other furnishings once lived within the room were a series of scratch marks cut deep into the hardwood floor in a jagged zigzag pattern—from the far end of the room, all the way to the door.

"Step back," the woman said. "Up against the wall, please."

Havoc and Gillette obeyed. Together they watched as the woman lifted the throw rug by a corner and folded it over, unveiling a double trap door underneath. Without losing momentum, she threw both doors open to reveal a descending staircase. Havoc tilted his neck to get a better look down below. He couldn't make out every detail, but the sub-level floor plan appeared to go on beyond the perimeter of the cathedral. Did all church buildings come this way—equipped with a subterranean shelter to hide out in when needed?

"Follow me, please," she said as she started her way down.

"Now wait just a second," Havoc protested. The woman stopped in her tracks and turned to face him. "While we appreciate you saving us from . . . from those things outside, we have no reason to trust you well enough to follow you down there. We don't even know your name for Christ's sake."

"My name isn't important at the moment," she told them. "All that matters, all that *should* matter, is our safety. But if you're going to allow yourselves to get hung up on something as trivial as knowing someone's name, then feel free to stay up here and pray our *hungry little friends* outside that door don't manage to find their way into this room." She stepped aside, waving them down. "Now, before we waste anymore time, follow me."

"But—"

"Don't make me say it a third time."

Gillette pushed Havoc toward the stairs, telling him it wasn't the time or place for such a discussion. And as they plunged into the unknown depths of the cathedral, with the floor level no longer cast in shadow, understated revelation overwhelmed the senses. Before them, as far as the eye could see, a seemingly endless layout of medical research equipment took up residence on every surface throughout the underground structure.

"What is this place?" Gillette asked.

"Originally, it started as a nine-tier, reinforced bomb shelter—designed and erected during the 1960s to house every citizen of Barstow, should the world fall victim to a nuclear holocaust. And according to public record, the cathedral above us was built only to conceal its existence until proven necessary; a promise for salvation against the fires of Hell."

"Excuse me," Havoc chimed in, "but did you say *nine-tier?*"

"I did. Lower levels and the southern subdivision of the first three floors were designated as housing establishments while the northern sections of those same first three served as our science and research department, which is where we currently find ourselves. Allow me to welcome you to the Lab, where everything eventually went south for all of us."

Havoc's attention fell to the floor. He suddenly felt weak in the knees. The thought of eight levels resting underneath his feet had turned his stomach with claustrophobia. Desperate for escape, he closed his eyes and focused on his breathing, hoping to wake up and find himself back in Paradise—with Gillette still sound asleep on the couch in her bedroom, the thought of traveling to Los Angeles still a pleasant daydream.

Unable to find solace with his thoughts, he wandered into the heart of the laboratory's first floor while the woman continued to tell the history of its troubled existence. And he couldn't believe his ears when she told them she was the only one left of its original 2,376 residents; that everyone else either fell victim to the infection, became someone's meal, or found themselves put to rest by the lower levels' containment measures to help prevent the contagion from spreading any further.

Nothing about tonight felt real.

# §4

---

# MOTHER & CHILD DIVIDED

"THE NAME'S ALLELE BY THE WAY, since you were insistent on knowing it for some reason," the woman said as she finished educating her unwanted visitors on the history of Barstow's horrific misfortune. "I would offer you both a room to rest for the night, but the original floor design for this level was reserved for those of us who worked up here; and the majority of levels four through nine are still considered . . . off limits."

Gillette motioned toward one of the smaller cubicles. "It's not a problem," she said. "We're used to sleeping on the ground and using whatever furniture we can find as makeshift beds."

"You said the lower levels are still off limits?"

"That is what I said, yes."

"Havoc." Gillette eyed her companion, begging him to keep quiet.

"It's fine," Allele reassured her. "I don't mind. A mild case of morbid curiosity never hurt anyone. Now, my dear boy—what about the term 'off limits' confuses you?"

"It's not the term itself, but the subtle pause that came before it."

"The subtle pause?"

"You sounded unsure of yourself on whether or not the term 'off limits' would *actually* discourage us from wanting to explore the lower levels, regardless of their status. That pause. It alone created its own subtext. It was as if another way to describe the condition of the lower levels—and a more honest one, at that—ran through your mind first, but then you faltered and made a last ditch effort to correct yourself mid-sentence; but the pause, that subtle pause, betrayed you."

Allele turned to Gillette. "Is he always like this?"

"To some degree, yeah—ever since we were kids."

"My condolences."

Ignoring their remarks, Havoc made his way to the other side of the room where a locked door branded by a bloody hand print stood; its sordid insignia appeared to be teasing him, begging to be opened. And to his left, another door stared him down. But unlike its adjacent twin, it remained unmarked—and when he checked, unlocked as well. He scanned the rest of the room, curious to find three more of the (he counted) six doorways found themselves stamped by the same crimson marker, leaving only two unblemished.

"Before you ask, because I have a feeling you will," Allele's voice echoed with condescension, "the answer is yes—only those two entryways remain open for access. And as previously stated, everywhere else is *off limits*; deemed unfit for exploration. So unless you feel like getting yourself killed tonight, I would recommend you heed every marked doorway's warning with extreme caution. They're there for a reason."

"I thought you said the lower levels' containment measures took care of everything," Gillette said, confused.

Allele sighed. "If only that were true." She marched her way across the room, joining Havoc at the blood-stained entrance and placed her left hand against its cold steel. "All the 'containment measures' managed to do was deplete the lower levels of their oxygen supply. While an effective tactic against those who had yet to be exposed, it had proven itself a fruitless effort against anyone already infected."

"What does that mean?" Havoc asked.

"Only the living require oxygen."

Allele's words hung in the air, haunting Gillette and Havoc to their core: *Only the living require oxygen.* Something about the way she said it allowed the phrase to linger long after the words themselves had faded into the background. It stayed at the forefront of their minds and continued to play on an endless loop, without their consent.

*Only the living require oxygen.*

Questions. In the end, that's all that remained: a tangled mess of unanswered questions. Havoc and Gillette didn't know where to begin. But with everything that had occurred since their arrival in the town of Barstow, the silence was starting to get to them. Living alone, while not ideal, didn't feel completely removed from the outside world when they caught a glimpse into Macro's way of life. Even in his solitude, Macro managed to find beauty through the art of photography—with the ability to shape the final outcome of every portrait to better suit his frame of mind. But here, in an underground laboratory, Allele had nothing to distract her from the unfortunate situation that surrounded her; how she managed to keep her wits about her the entire time a mystery to them both.

"How did this all happen?"

"Consider it poor judgment on my behalf." Allele choked as the words left her tongue. "Misplaced confidence on a specific neural treatment I had spent half a decade in research and development that, in hindsight, wasn't ready for clinical testing. But when you're desperate to find a solution, with time running out at a startling pace, you'll find yourself making one brash decision after another. And when the subtle signs of failure begin to rise to the surface, the act of denial will do all it can to bury the truth for as long as one can manage, to keep it like a secret until it's too late to undo the damage, leaving you with only a mountain of regret to sort through long after the rest of the world has crumbled at your feet."

"But if you're the only one left alive," Gillette commented, trying to piece it all together, "then why don't you just leave?"

Allele's gaze fell inward, her stature withdrawn. A sadness filled her eyes as she searched for a response. "While I may be the only survivor of this epidemic," her eyes studied a piece of string tied to her left ring finger, "that doesn't mean I have nothing keeping me here."

"I'm not sure I understand," Havoc said.

"Even if what happened here managed to take away everything I held dear in my life before it all came to an unfortunate end," again, she continued to examine her left hand, "I've found it impossible to divorce myself from the associations to those who were taken from me." Her attention eventually left the twine on her finger and returned to the blood-stained door where her hand rested. A single tear fell down her cheek. "Even if all that remains is my memory of what they *used to be*, I would never forgive myself if I chose to abandon them to this godforsaken place . . . to be forgotten by the world. They deserve better. They should be remembered."

Havoc watched as Allele's composure continued to decline. All the silent sentiments, the pain in her voice when she spoke, the otherwise trivial details of the framed photograph he saw upstairs; he understood her reason for staying. It was a similar reason he had used to explain why he had stayed in Paradise for as long as he did, even after he had learned how to drive. He feared the act of leaving would somehow minimize the impact the small town had on his upbringing. And even with the promise he made to himself as a child, to continue his journey out to the coast, he didn't want to leave the memory of his father behind. Because other than the car, Paradise was all Havoc had left as a gentle reminder of his existence.

"Saying goodbye is never easy." He placed a hand on Allele's shoulder, hoping to comfort her. "Believe me, I know. I've lost someone close to me, as well. You'll do anything and everything to keep their memory alive for as long as possible, but it'll get to a point where the very notion becomes more a detriment to your well-being than its original intention. . . . It's okay to let go." He paused, wondering if his words were having any effect. "It may feel wrong, but those we loved wouldn't want us to quit living on their behalf. Your son wouldn't—"

"How did you know I have a son?" Allele asked defensively.

"I noticed the photograph of you two upstairs."

Allele smiled. "Betrayed by my own pathos, I guess."

"You had a son?" Gillette chimed in, feeling left out of the conversation. She studied every doorway with a bloody hand print on it, curious to know which one led to his makeshift catacomb. "How old was he when everything—"

"He'll be eleven next spring."

"A fun age, I'm sure."

"What was his name?" Havoc asked.

"Vector," she said, warm nostalgia in her voice. "His father named him; a playful attempt at biological humor. And the irony isn't lost to me with everything that's happened this past month."

A quiet moment befell them. From above and below, the sound of footsteps and feral outcries echoed to fill the void. Having been preoccupied by the casual sway of conversation, lost in a dialogue of past participles, the threat that surrounded them from every angle had fallen into the background; its haunting choreography an unwanted composition to everyone's ears as it resurfaced, becoming a relentless drone of shuffling syncopation.

"Do you think Vector would have wanted you to stay here on his behalf, to die in this place along with him?"

"You're asking me to leave my son behind, and that is something I simply cannot do." Another tear fell, joining its predecessor. "Even if all what used to make him my little Vector is gone from his eyes, and only a monster remained, I don't believe I would ever have the strength to leave him; the bond between a mother and child . . . you'd be asking the impossible from me."

While it pained Havoc to take in Allele's words of surrender, he respected her decision. If Gillette were to share the same fate as poor Vector, he would have felt a similar disposition toward such a notion, unable to leave her to the depths of an underground hellscape.

"I've come to terms with dying in a place ruled by the tormented sounds of silence," she said. "We may not be able to erase every blemish created by our past mistakes, but as long as my conscience remains free from the guilt of abandoning those I love, I'll be able to leave this world peacefully—be it due to starvation, infection, or some other unfortunate means; whatever the cause, I welcome it."

Havoc and Gillette both fell silent shortly after Allele expressed her unshakable desire to join the rest of Barstow when the time came for her. She considered her fate a fair punishment, a reprimand for her attempt to rewrite the inevitable. And she laughed at the nuanced sense of whimsy the world possessed: a scientific institution buried under a house of God, its discoveries doomed to be eternally squandered and suppressed at every turn, forced to remain nothing more than a minor misstep in human ingenuity.


APPEARING CALM AND COLLECTED, Allele left the static comfort of the door's cold exterior. Havoc watched as she ambled down the aisles and let the room consume her, finding it impossible to believe that, only a little over a month ago, the place still breathed life throughout its many levels—how different their visit would have been had they passed through before its eventual downfall, and the swarm of shamblers moving around upstairs didn't help his imagination.

"It sounds as if they've made the cathedral their new home," Allele said, somewhat amused.

"What does that mean?" Gillette asked.

Allele turned to face her, a cold and calculated stare across her face. "It means if you wish to leave this place at some point, we'll have to make our way through the first floor's residential area in order to get to the main entrance."

"Sounds simple enough," Havoc said as he examined every entryway, wondering which one they would have to go through, hoping it was one of the unmarked ones. "Which way will we be heading?"

"Look behind you."

Havoc's gaze returned to the door where he still stood, its bloodstained marker staring him down, mocking him. A knot formed in his stomach. He gripped the butt of his revolver, but found little comfort from its presence. Silently, he counted the ammunition still locked in its cylinder and felt the metal casings of each round around his waist, wondering if it would be enough.

"What should we expect on the other side?"

"I think you already know."

# §5

# A MAZE OF DEATH

VIOLENT APPREHENSION weighed on everyone's minds as they prepared for what lay ahead, the extent to whatever horrors awaited them beyond the door's threshold an unknown factor. Allele convinced Havoc and Gillette to ditch the shopping cart for a pair of knapsacks to carry their essentials the rest of the way, that the cart would only become a hindrance once they reached the residential area's narrowed hallways.

"Are you sure we can't wait until sunrise?" Gillette asked, her voice shaking. "Didn't you say those things are nocturnal?"

"Do you see any windows around that would help delineate a day-or-night cycle to anyone living down here?"

"It was only a question."

"Do you?"

"No."

"Then it's not going to matter when we leave," Allele said. "Without any indication of night or day, a shambler won't feel the need to rest or hide from the sun. It'll roam down every corridor looking for some form of sustenance until its body decomposes beyond practical function or it starves to death — the latter being the more likely of the two outcomes."

"Why do you say that?" a curious Havoc inquired.

"Remember when I said only the living require oxygen?"

"It never left my thoughts."

"Without oxygen," Allele continued, "or the presence of bacteria or fungi, the body doesn't know the proper notion of decay. Whatever still *lives* on the other side of that door will have not been subjected to the same level of decomposition like the ones above us have. They will move faster and have the ability to be more aggressive than their outdoor counterparts."

"You said you depleted every residential level of its air supply, yes?"

"That's correct."

"Then why don't you flood the route we're about to take with oxygen again so their bodies begin to fall apart?"

"Even if I could, it doesn't work that quickly. Decomp can take months or years, depending on the living conditions of the corpse."

"What do you mean by *Even if you could?*" Gillette asked.

"There's simply not enough oxygen in the Lab's reserve tanks to revitalize the lower levels to full capacity, let alone a select subdivision. And until tonight, I've been relying on fresh air from the surface to help keep this area somewhat inhabitable."

Havoc turned to face the trap door where they had entered from the backroom of the cathedral. He imagined it being swarmed by a mindless horde of shamblers as they shuffled around aimlessly, wondering where their late-night snack had wandered off to as the scent of fresh meat lingered on their noses. And if it weren't for their intrusion, had they sought shelter in another building all together, Allele could have continued living her life in silence—to quietly mourn the extended loss of her husband and son without interruption. Instead, she would find herself forced to face her demons all over again, to witness the weight of her actions head-on and carry the burden across her shoulders from one end of an underground labyrinth and back before being given the chance to rest

He did not envy her current position.

Gillette left the comfort of Allele's shadow and joined Havoc at the foot of the marked doorway, unable to fathom what atrocities lurked beyond the steel obstruction; getting out of Barstow alive remained her only concern. Her only distraction rested near the center of her chest. She could feel her heart pounding.

"But if the path we're about to take is still without any oxygen, then how are we supposed to make the journey to the other end of the complex?" she asked. "Last I checked, Havoc and I weren't known for holding our breath for an extended period of time."

"I've got that covered," Allele said as she disappeared under one of the tables for a quick second—coming back up with three cylindrical containers. "Diatomic O2 tanks. They should hold us over for the entire trip."

"You don't sound one-hundred percent certain about that," Havoc remarked. "Any reason why they wouldn't?"

"That all depends on the user's ability to make every breath count. In theory, the tank should never run out of oxygen. But if the person using the equipment takes one too many rapid breaths at a time, it won't be able to filter and convert the $CO_2$ our lungs expel back into reusable oxygen, leaving the individual at risk of passing out. And if you pass out in a room occupied by a horde of shamblers, I can guarantee you won't live long enough to wake back up."

"So take deep breaths and release each one slowly, got it," Gillette said as she took a tank from Allele. "That should be easy enough to remember." The canister, small in size, fit snug in a side pocket on her knapsack. She watched Havoc go through the same motions, securing his lifeline for the journey ahead. And in unplanned unison, they tested their tank's function: a deep inhale, followed by a measured and controlled exhale. Together they repeated the process, feeling the effects of breathing recycled oxygen.

Pleased by their results with the diatomic O2 containers, Allele sauntered back to join her two guests and waved her hand over a side panel to reveal a keypad. "Whatever happens beyond this point," she said as she entered a six digit code, "remember to stay calm and maintain as steady a breathing rhythm as you can."

A low-registered beep confirmed access as the automated door slid to the left and disappeared into the wall. Beyond its threshold existed a small room—wide and long enough to fit no more than four people comfortably within its parameters. And on the other side, a second steel door blocked their way. Allele motioned them inside and followed behind Gillette as the door slithered closed; pressurized steam and a dry heat filled the room shortly after.

Once the steam and hot air finished their cycle the door ahead of them opened, welcoming them to the residential area. But the welcome was short-lived when Allele shined a flashlight ahead to help light their way.

All along the corridor a mess of mangled corpses lined the floor, as far as Allele's flashlight would allow them to see, their lacerated silhouettes a mass produced spectacle tailored to offend the senses. Havoc paused to redirect his and Gillette's attention elsewhere, hoping to spare her from the morbid scene a moment longer—the ceiling her only sanctuary. But the image had already invaded Havoc's consciousness, and no change of scenery could save him.

"I never thought I would find myself walking through this part of the complex again," Allele said; a breath of nostalgia painted her words with a shade of melancholy. Her pace slowed to remember the

way things were before, her memory failing her. "Life used to occupy these halls with such hope. We dreamed of the day we could rebuild the world from the ground up—erase its dark history from our collective memory. We wanted to believe in a better future for generations to come, that humanity's narrative didn't end when the bombs fell. But if this past month has proven anything to me, it's that self-realized extinction is hardwired into our DNA."

Unable to hold his gaze toward the ceiling, Havoc's attention fell to the floor. He held Gillette's hand and continued to guide her through the maze of death. The bodies reminded him of those from topside, their remains picked apart by a family of vultures. But he knew no such wildlife lived underground, that something once considered human had gnawed its way through the flesh of another. He wondered what the relationship between corpse and shambler had been beforehand. And if any semblance of humanity remained buried within the core of the now undead's mental faculties, did they hesitate at all before biting down on their fallen companion?

"Okay. We'll have to be quiet from here on out," Allele said, her voice just above a whisper.

Before Havoc could ask why his eyes met the sight ahead. A small unit of the infected roamed among the chewed remnants of Barstow's citizens, looking for food. He felt himself begin to panic, his breathing no longer subdued and deliberate but shallow and rapid. The chilled presence of Gillette's hand within his helped to calm him, but he could still feel his heart racing. Because unlike those he had witnessed on the surface, whose state of decay aided in their portrayal as something less than human, their subterranean brethren appeared supernatural. And if it weren't for the circle of carmine dripping from their lips and a white cloud living where a shade of blue or green or brown once resided, he would have been unable to tell them apart from a random passerby making their way through Paradise on a supply run before they carried on with their journey, heading east or west.

And in the darkened silence, with only their footsteps to serve as background noise, he swore he could hear them speaking to one another on occasion, voicing their hunger as the search continued.

*"Is it someone new?"*

*"And the one from before."*

*"The one who did this to us."*

Havoc froze when he saw three of them rise from an already scavenged meal. His instincts dictated he let go of Gillette's hand and reach for his revolver. But he remembered he only had five shots left before he would have to reload, and he feared he wouldn't have enough time to do so before another wave of shamblers stumbled from around the corner and overcame him. Still frozen in place, he watched as they wandered down the corridor toward their location, not a shuffle in their step. They felt the air in front of them, feeling for any change in the surrounding temperature.

Gillette's gaze left the ceiling, seeing the horror in front of them. "Can they see us?" she asked.

"They can," Allele said, her attention still ahead. She placed the flashlight against her shoulder and fished a handful of shotgun shells from her lab coat and loaded them into her 12 gauge. She turned and handed Havoc the light. "Get ready to run, you two. It's about to get loud and they're going to be attracted to the sound of gunshots. If any of them get too close, shine the torch in their eyes. It'll blind them long enough for you to get away."

"What if—"

"And if you can manage to get a shot in, aim for the head."

"But what if we get separated? How will Gillette and I know which way to go?"

Ignoring the question, Allele stormed down the hallway, meeting the three approaching shamblers halfway to greet them with a quick barrage of gunfire; all three fell before she could expel the third shotgun shell. Witnessing such a violent onslaught a second time terrified

Havoc. It troubled him, the number of times she must've found herself forced to execute the same savage act to be able to follow through with it with such fluid precision. He wondered if her son—or even if her husband—had been on the receiving end at some point.

Distant cries echoed throughout the entire complex from every direction, filled with rage and hunger.

"Quick, we don't have much time," Allele said, already leading them down the main hallway as she reloaded her weapon. "Follow me and don't look back—just focus on reaching the other side."

"How much farther do we have to go?" Gillette asked.

"A few twists and turns here and there, but it's not far. That is if my memory hasn't failed me, of course."

They continued down the main corridor until they reached a dead end. Allele looked both ways before she turned right. The layout of the place confused Havoc as he and Gillette followed their guide toward their supposed exit; with every bend they traveled down, the less it all made sense. Everything, every corridor and doorway, looked and felt indistinguishable from what had come before it. How anyone managed to find their way through such a labyrinth . . . to linger on it only served to confuse him further. *Just focus on getting out of here*, he reminded himself. *And remember to steady your breathing. You don't want to pass out down here.*

*Only the living require oxygen.*


AFTER RUNNING FOR WHAT FELT like an eternity, Allele stopped suddenly; an act which caused a two-part collision when Havoc ran into her, and Gillette into him shortly after. Concerned, Havoc shined the flashlight ahead to see what forced Allele to stop dead in her tracks.

Before them, at the foot of the stairs which led to the surface, with his back to them, stood a small boy—no older than ten or eleven, his ghostly silhouette bathed in the red afterglow of an EXIT sign hanging above him. Havoc's light stayed on the boy, waiting for Allele to make the next move. But only a word escaped her lips:

*Vector.*

The child turned to face them, his eyes white like all the others. Dried crimson stained his lips and the tattered remains of his shirt. A pained sensation turned in Havoc's stomach when he saw the child's face—to know he had once been a normal, loving son to Allele and his father; and to imagine the heartache it caused her to see him this way, knowing he would never be the same.

"Mom . . . Mommy?" the boy struggled to say.

"It's me, Sweetie," Allele choked, fighting tears. She lowered her weapon and got down on her knees. "I'm here."

"*I . . . I feel sick, Mommy.*"

"I know you do, but Mommy is here now to make it all better." She held her arms open. "Just let me hold you. Do you remember how I used to hold you and make your bad feelings go away?"

The boy bared his teeth. "*No . . . shots.*"

"No more shots, I promise." Allele reassured him. She turned to face Havoc and Gillette. "When he's no longer guarding the stairs, you two need to make a run for it."

Havoc nodded and then looked to Gillette, to make sure she understood the plan as well. But all Gillette could do was continue to stand and stare at the young boy as he made his slow approach toward Allele, unable to believe the scene playing before her very eyes.

"Come here, Sweetie. It's going to be okay. Everything is going to be all right."

Despite his condition, it didn't take long for the boy to make contact with his mother, leaving the pathway to the exit clear. The two stared into each other's eyes for a moment, Allele remembering every memory she had of him while Vector edged a step closer to the woman he had once shared a heartbeat with, both desperate to rekindle what had been lost to them for well over a month. And together they embraced as mother and child had many countless times before, with his ear on her right shoulder, their arms wrapped around each other for the first time in what must've felt like forever. Letting go with her unarmed hand, and with a subtle wave, Allele motioned for Havoc and Gillette to make their move toward the stairs.

"*I love you, Mom . . . Mommy.*"

"I love you too, Sweetheart." Her voice had become fragile, the words barely audible—meant only for his ears. Using all the energy she had left in her, Allele raised the shotgun and positioned it against the side of her son's head, tilting the barrel to her right. "Nothing can or will hurt you anymore; you have my word."

She pulled the trigger.

Havoc and Gillette watched as both mother and son fell to the floor, still embracing one another—one final act of love. A crippling sadness overcame them, keeping them in place . . . a desire to mourn the sudden loss. But they couldn't stay; the walls of the complex were no longer safe, having become lost to the screams of hunger.

"Gill, we better go," Havoc finally spoke. He took hold of her hand and led her toward the exit—to greet the surface as one would an old friend. And as the door closed behind them, neither one of them had the strength to look back and say goodbye.

# CHAPTER 4

## WHERE WE BELONG

# §1

## THE MOURNING AFTER

DAYLIGHT HAD YET TO SHINE DOWN on the cold California desert, but unfettered adrenaline pushed Havoc and Gillette to their limit until the walking nightmare of Barstow was behind them; survival their only concern, the thought of wildlife crossing their path no longer a threat. All that mattered was getting to the next town and hoping for the best. And even when the sun finally traded places with the moon, Havoc's hand never left Gillette's. It felt safe there; a tangible reminder—his way of knowing she was still with him.

By high noon exhaustion had taken over, the lack of sleep having caught up with them.

"Havoc," Gillette said through parched lips.

"Yeah?"

"How much farther do we have?"

Havoc shrugged as he shielded his eyes from the sun to look ahead, but everything in his line of view looked near-identical to what had come before it; the occasional roadside marker stating the distance until the next two-to-three towns the only way to mark their progress. Another mile disappeared beneath their feet before he could make out the finer details of an approaching street sign on the horizon, its white letters barely legible on the wall of faded green: HESPERIA 17. A sigh of relief escaped him, knowing they were close to finding sanctuary, and praying it didn't hide any untold horrors underneath its infrastructure—not after what he and Gillette witnessed in Barstow.

"By the look of it, not much farther."

"Then can we please rest for a bit? My feet are killing me."

Havoc nodded. He would never admit it, but he felt the same level of exhaustion she did. But more than fatigue plagued her eyes. Unanticipated grief weighed heavily on their minds. He found it confusing, to not only feel the desire to mourn the loss of someone he knew less than a day but to also grieve the death of a child he had known for mere minutes—a young life stripped of opportunity before it had been given a chance to breathe. But the final image of a mother holding what remained of her son before pulling the trigger on them both had become an unwanted loop of traumatic memory. And even with the incident now in their rear-view mirror, with retrospect on their side, nothing about last night made sense. All Havoc and Gillette could do to help clear their thoughts of such an ordeal was to focus on the deed at hand: eat and rest for a quick minute before pressing forward to the next town.


LOST IN A COLD CAN OF BEANS, Havoc let the weight of his surroundings consume him—felt the warmth of the sun beating down on him while a delicate breeze dusted souvenirs across his skin. It felt familiar, reminded him of his life in Paradise; comfort found him with its sub-tleties. He never would have imagined he'd wind up missing the place where he grew up—the associations affiliated with desert sand's abrasive nature.

Still, he welcomed the sensation.

"Do you think we made a mistake?" Gillette asked.

"A mistake?" Havoc stopped mid-bite and turned to find Gillette had stopped eating all together. He followed her eyes, curious to know where her thoughts had carried off to, but her elusive gaze wandered across the entirety of California's desolate landscape—unable to focus on anything long enough to keep her mind from drifting. "I'm not sure I understand. What are you trying to say?"

"You don't feel it, too?" she said, confused. "I mean, after what we've just been through, how could you not?" She placed her can of beans off to the side, her appetite lost. "You were right to say what you did a couple of nights ago. This entire trip has been one nightmare after another. And after our time in Barstow, it has me worried. What if it only gets worse from here on out?"

Gillette's eyes met his. While unresolved anger rested on the surface of her irises, a sadness lived underneath their hardened exterior. Any sense of optimism and wonder had faded from their emerald complexion; not even the light from the sun could bring them back to life. He couldn't fault her for the sudden shift in disposition, having witnessed the same horrendous sequence play itself out. Watching someone die already carried an unwelcome weight to one's shoulders, but to experience the act in such a violent way—to see someone do themselves in alongside their own flesh and blood—demanded its own place in the world, and it could never be forgotten.

He wanted to comfort her, tell her the worst was behind them, but knew his words would get him nowhere, that all he could do was sit and watch as she continued to lose herself to whatever plagued her. It troubled him to know his limitations, to acknowledge the inability to distract and help pull a dear friend from such a paralyzing state; the only sentiment left available to him that could calm her was to reach out and place his hand on her shoulder, letting her know she wasn't alone with her feelings.

"We're never going to find our way back home, are we?" Her voice trembled under the weight of trauma. "At least not on foot anyway. Because unless we manage to find a salvageable vehicle to use somewhere along the way—which, given the lack of foot traffic we've seen so far along the highway, feels unlikely—Paradise might as well be lost to us; a memory from our past . . . nothing more."

Havoc sighed. His attention ventured to the east, Gillette's last remark having stayed with him. "All we can do is hope for the best," he said. "If all else fails, we can try and make a life for ourselves on the coast. If not in Los Angeles, we can always travel north until we find a place we both like well enough to settle down in." He lifted his gaze to greet the sun, knowing it would soon start its descent into the western mountains. "We should probably get moving again soon if we plan on making it to the next town before nightfall."

A wooden, unimpressed stare met him when he turned back to face Gillette. He could still sense a layer of defeat weighing her down, but it didn't keep her from collecting herself and joining him to continue their trek.


AS THEY CONTINUED DOWN the Interstate, Havoc marveled at the scope of their surroundings. Unlike countless descriptions he had read in books back home, where monuments and skyscrapers occupied the character's field of view, untamed beauty had claimed the skyline in every direction: the smile of every mountain peak on the horizon a welcome departure from the stream of cacti and Joshua trees nearby. While not foreign to his senses, with a similar spectacle waiting for him in Paradise, the scenery before him sang a different tune—one of nostalgia without regret. Its existence carried no ulterior motive; it only served as a silent reminder, of the way things used to be. *Such simplicity should be remembered forever.*

The thought carried itself into action as Havoc retrieved the Polaroid camera from his knapsack and aimed its artificial eye at the mountainous terrain ahead and took a snapshot. His attention to detail paled in comparison to Macro's artistic ability, but he could learn to cherish its imperfections; nothing could diminish its impact. It would continue to remind him to remain optimistic, even when the world revealed itself as something less than beautiful.

"After the grief you gave Macro about photography, I'm surprised to see you using that thing," Gillette said. "See something you like?"

Havoc smiled and angled the camera in her direction and blindly took another picture. He let Gillette's question hang in the air, leaving it unanswered. His focus lingered on his most recent photograph as the image developed in his hand. A brief moment in time—no longer present, but now forever a part of the past—had become more than just a memory. And as the miles continued to pass beneath their feet, he would glance at its rectangular frame; its candid nature, the way he managed to capture Gillette's personality on film, with the California mountains complimenting her in the background, never ceased to amaze him.


A SENSE OF SERENITY GREETED THEM as they edged closer to their destination. Among the city's lifeless architecture, a human element existed. While its urban skyline carried little personality with it, it reminded Havoc of Paradise; even the subtle colors of the sun setting on the horizon painted the city's silhouette with a shade of familiarity. He welcomed the thought of arriving in a town absent of any demons.

Gillette held her arm out to stop them, her hand shaking.

"What's wrong?" he asked.

"How do we know it's safe?"

"We don't. But with the threat of nightfall only minutes away, do we really have a choice?" The words were meant to comfort her, but the look in Gillette's eyes remained the same—an unshakable sense of worry weighing them down. He took hold of her hand and let it rest on his chest, letting her feel his heartbeat. "I'm scared, too. But if we don't find shelter soon, who knows what might find us in the middle of the night. We need our rest, and the town up ahead is our best bet. Barstow may have been a nightmare, but it's behind us now."

"Is it though?" The words felt brittle as they left her lips, their foundation devoid of certainty.

Havoc turned his gaze back to the city, its peaceful outline inviting. Looks could be deceiving, he knew that much, but he refused to let past experience pass judgment on a town that had done nothing to wrong him. Still holding Gillette's hand, he led them into the city limits of Hesperia. A prayer left his lips in a whisper, hoping such optimism wouldn't prove itself a foolish pursuit.

He wanted to believe the worst was over.


A COOL EVENING BREEZE CARRIED THEM the rest of the way, every subsequent step less apprehensive than its predecessor. It helped to watch and hear the town come to life as they continued their approach. Weightless conversation floated from every open window, not a breath of dissidence in the air; everything about its composition a welcoming change of pace. Even in the dark of night the sound of children's laughter could be heard outside, any semblance of fear for the desert's wildlife nowhere to be found. The entire city—this small corner of the world—felt at peace with itself, completely removed from anything that might wish to cause harm to its citizens.

Consumed by the surrounding atmosphere, Gillette's hand left the comfort of Havoc's grip. She wandered toward the town's center, her ears drawn to the playful screams of delectation. Havoc followed after her, his own curiosity piqued.

The children stopped playing when they noticed two strangers approaching them. Most of them ran and disappeared through the doorway of their homes, leaving only a handful behind; their eyes wide with a curiosity of their own.

"Can we help you?" the oldest one asked, her voice timid. The others remained silent, too scared to move.

Gillette explained their situation. She left out the finer details of their time in Barstow, telling them they were heading west toward the coast and had experienced issues with their car her main focus. The children stood and stared, interrupting her with a question here and there, fascinated by what little she told them about their previous town. The entire exchange reminded Havoc of when he and Gillette were their age. He remembered every stranger that ever passed through Paradise growing up, the stories they told from back home while Ford topped off their fuel tank outside his grocery store. He never imagined the day would come when *he* would be the passing stranger in an unfamiliar town, entertaining the neighborhood children with tales of other cities, igniting their sense of wonder to one day leave their hometown for sights unseen. He hoped when their time came—to venture out into the world as adults—their experience on the road and away from home would prove itself something worth looking back on fondly.

"But what we need is a place to stay for a day or two," Gillette said. "The last place we passed through didn't offer us a moment to rest and we're both exhausted."

The children turned and looked at each other, a silent exchange comprised of directionless shrugs and hand gestures. Havoc and Gillette watched and waited while they worked out a solution. It reminded them of when they were kids, their ability to communicate with each other in complete silence through the use of body language, and how it would annoy Gillette's father at the dinner table whenever they refrained from speaking for an entire evening. Havoc smiled at the childhood memory as he watched it play itself out before him through a younger generation.

"If you don't mind sharing a room," the youngest of the three finally spoke, "We wouldn't mind asking our father if you could use his study for a couple of nights."

"We wouldn't want to intrude," Havoc said.

"Please," the oldest remarked. "The old man hardly uses the room as it is. It's just a place to keep his books so momma didn't have to see them all about the house anymore. Other than a means for storage, we forget that room exists half the time."

Havoc exchanged a brief glance with Gillette. The children's offer appeared promising, and the notion of sharing a room wasn't foreign to them. And after last night, the thought of sleeping in separate rooms didn't sit well in their stomachs. Not even the apparent blanket of security Hesperia provided by its withdrawn presence from the rest of the Wasteland could convince them to spend an evening apart.

# §2

## A MARK OF AFFECTION

AS THE CHILDREN LED THEM away from the town's center, toward the residential area, the feeling of familiarity continued to pervade Havoc's senses. Everywhere he looked reminded him of Paradise. *But in the dark, everything feels familiar,* his mind echoed. First impressions often deceive and he refused to believe such a place existed—a place that could feel like home.

Exhausted from the day's journey, Havoc let his head fall back to watch the moon and the stars loom over the city as the air of Hesperia carried them forward. And with his head lost in the clouds, his ears danced to the sound of a wind chime performing a haphazard melody somewhere in the distance.

"It's rare for us to have visitors," the oldest child said. "People tend to just pass us by on their way to or from the coastal cities. So what exactly brings you two all the way out here from the Nevadan desert? If it's to see the ocean I'll tell you this: Once you've seen one body of water, you've pretty much seen them all."

While neither Havoc or Gillette understood the girl's attempt at humor, the younger children laughed at the joke's obscure punchline without restraint.

"How far are we from the ocean?" Gillette asked.

"That depends."

"On what, exactly?"

"Which town you want to drive through to get there. Most of the southern coast is completely abandoned, so traffic shouldn't be a problem. But if you're making your way through Los Angeles, you might want to visit the Pier at some point."

"The Pier?"

"An over-sized playground," the youngest one blurted out in excitement. "Laney almost made it to the top once, but then Father found us and told her to come down—said it was dangerous, that Laney could've gotten hurt if she had climbed any higher."

Havoc chuckled at the little one's interjection. It reminded him of Gillette when she was her age, when she used to interrupt her father mid-sentence to express herself without pause—how every word found itself underpinned by a layer of emphasis as they left her tongue. *It's strange*, he thought. How the personality of a complete stranger could remind him of someone he had known his entire life.


EVERYONE'S MOOD CHANGED when they arrived at their destination. Laney and her younger siblings traded expressions, silently determining their course of action upon opening the front door. They all turned their attention to Havoc and Gillette, their eyes awash with uncomfortable uncertainty. The middle child mentioned they had never brought strangers to the house before and were worried their father might turn them away. But his eyes told a different story. While his words spoke of worry, his eyes were dressed with fear.

"Marshall, you're being paranoid," Laney remarked. "These days, Dad is more bark than bite and you know it." She turned her attention to her two guests. "The old man may appear intimidating at first, but he's got a good heart. And worst case scenario, Mom will step in and put him in his place. There's nothing to—"

Before Laney could finish her final thought, the door opened. The sharp exposure to artificial light blinded everyone; the shadow of someone small-framed stood before them, blocking the entrance. No imminent threat existed from the individual's sudden appearance, but it didn't prevent Havoc's thoughts from reliving last night's events: the slow approach of the shamblers after they rose from their motionless state, the vacant look in their eyes; he could still hear their tortured groans as they searched for something to eat. Tension built in his chest. He breathed and counted to four, hoping to calm his nerves before his anxiety got the better of him.

"Now if I had known you three were going to bring company home with you," the shadow finally spoke, "I would have left dinner out a little while longer." The woman's tone of voice alone decorated her words with a smile.

"Travelers from somewhere back east," Laney said as she pushed past her mother. "They approached us looking for a place to stay for a couple of nights and we kind off offered up Dad's study as a makeshift bedroom to sleep in while they rested. I hope that's okay."

"Your father may have issue with it at first, but I'm sure I'll be able to talk him into the idea." She stepped aside to let the rest of them in, winking at Havoc and Gillette as they entered. "So somewhere back east, huh? Where about?"

"Not that far, honestly," Havoc answered. "Just a small town in Southern Nevada, nothing special."

"Off to see the coast, I'm guessing," the woman continued with a smile. She turned to close the door behind her. "And since it's just the two of you, is it safe to presume you're are on a getaway of sorts — a honeymoon, perhaps? I mean, what other reason would two youngins such as yourselves be doing traveling to the ocean for?"

Nervous laughter left Havoc's lips. He turned to find the mother's attention had stayed with him. Her eyes lingered, studying his body language for anything resembling an attempt to hide his emotions. He held his breath and returned the sentiment, not fond of feeling he had been placed under a lens of subatomic scrutiny.

"It's nothing like that," he finally said. "We're just friends — two friends who thought it would be a good idea to travel through the desert and see the city of Los Angeles."

"Laney told them to make a stop at the Pier while out that way," the youngest child screamed from another room.

"Willow! What the hell?"

The mother smiled and laughed at her children's sudden descent into madness. A routine evening in their home she would tell Havoc and Gillette as she led them to their room, offering them a bite to eat from the kitchen before turning in; she directed a subtle wink in Havoc's direction before closing the door.

The room itself appeared how the children had described it: a place for storage. Trinkets from the past lined the study, its atmosphere more akin to a time capsule than a living space. And on the far wall, a family of bookcases touched the ceiling, their shelves stacked to the brim with the written word; their spines cracked and well-worn, Havoc could barely make out some of their titles. The sight reminded him of the conversation he had with Ford the day before he left Paradise.

"At least there's a couch," Gillette pointed out. She ambled toward it and made herself at home on its cushions; a breath of relief left her lips as she sank into its comforting pull.

"I almost forgot to tell you," the mother said as she came back into the room. "If it gets too cold during the night, there should be a few blankets in one of the armoires for you to use." She let her words settle in the air for a moment, waiting for a response to come from one of her guests, but both Havoc and Gillette remained silent. "Now rest easy, you two. Breakfast will be ready in the morning. And if you need anything in the middle of the night, Gibson and I are in the next room." She smiled and closed the door behind her.

THE ROOM'S MESS OF MEMORABILIA continued to stare Havoc and Gillette down as they settled into their surroundings. It all screamed to be sorted through, every detail of their inanimate existence scrutinized to the point of exhaustion, but they denied such temptation. They considered their desperate desire to leave the world behind for a dream or two for the rest of the evening a far more appealing means of escape; any inkling of curiosity could wait until morning.

With the lights off and his eyes closed, Havoc allowed his thoughts to wander. He enjoyed the quiet reprieve of lying on the floor, his attention lost to all the non-existent shapes and constellations he would often find in the ceiling while he waited for sleep to find him. But tonight his mind traveled elsewhere; he found himself remembering his childhood, recalling what few memories still remained.

He pictured his mother sitting in front of the vanity in her bedroom as she curled her hair into ceramic rollers, the faint notes of a melody floating softly through the air as she hummed a tune only familiar to her. And while most of his memories had fallen to the wayside through the years, having been replaced by more recent ones, the sound of his mother's voice had stayed with him.

"Havoc?"

Shaken from his thoughts, Havoc turned to meet Gillette's gaze. Even if she tried to hide it in the darkness of night, he could sense fear and sadness in her eyes.

"What is it?" he asked.

"Do you mind if I join you?"

Her question left him dumbstruck. It had been years since they last slept so close together. He knew the reason why and he couldn't fault her for wanting to join him on the floor. She feared the sight of Allele and Vector would haunt her the second she closed her eyes; the sound of the shotgun blast resonating through her mind, and the unspeakable consequence that followed.

It was the raid all over again.

Without exchanging words, Havoc pulled his blanket aside to welcome her on the floor beside him. A breath of hesitation colored her motions with unnerved delicacy, afraid any other speed would expose vulnerability on her part. But any false pretense disappeared the moment her head struck the pillow; tears fell, her eyes no longer capable of repressing such emotions. Havoc remained silent. Having learned from the night after the raid, he knew not to attempt to comfort her with words. Instead, he surrendered the room to Gillette—to fill with the sounds of mourning; laying his arm across her stomach his only gesture of consolation.

But among the muted sniffles of Gillette's unexpected grief, Havoc felt her hand on his, her fingers finding peace as they slowly became intertwined with his own.


"HAVOC?" GILLETTE SAID, her voice just above a whisper. "Are you still awake?" She turned to face him, his eyes still wide open; their icy shade of blue illuminated by the moon's pale glow—undisturbed by her question.

"Have yet to sleep a wink," he replied. "What's up?"

"Can you promise me something?"

"What is it?"

"No matter what happens—" She cut herself short, a wave of doubt in the way she spoke. "—if the day ever comes where I'm no longer around, promise me you won't allow yourself to feel a pain similar to what Allele went through when she lost Vector and everyone else she cared for."

"You know I can't guarantee that," he said.

"Why not?"

"Because that's not how human emotions work, Gill. You and I have a history, one that goes back to when we were still capable of losing ourselves to our imaginations—where we could pretend the floor was lava or boiling acid and the layout of the movie theater had become that of an ancient castle, where one of us would cry out for the other to come rescue us. Such shared memories will link us together until we're both gone from this world. Your hypothetical absence, however sudden and prolonged it may turn out to be, could never erase them, even if I wanted them gone. And with them there to haunt me, pain will find its way to my soul—without fail—whenever I decide to look back, knowing no new memories will ever be created."

"Just promise me you'll continue to live your life to the fullest after I'm gone, okay?"

"Don't talk like that. You're not going anywhere anytime soon."

"Will you just promise me?"

"Okay."

Quiet solemnity occupied the space between them. Together they lay tirelessly on the floor, unable to find sleep, their minds running rampant with such unwelcome thoughts. Havoc offered to read until they passed out, but Gillette declined; she lied and said the silence didn't bother her.

The sound of a wind chime dancing outside to the rhythm of the wind carried a soft lullaby into the room, eventually suspending their eyelids, allowing them to sleep and dream—Havoc's arm still wrapped around Gillette for comfort.

# §3

## VIENNA-LITE

AVOC OPENED HIS EYES to greet the colors of an approaching sunrise. A family of voices could be heard in the background, their broken melody playing throughout the house. He dropped his gaze to find Gillette still sound asleep. He smiled, pleased to see she managed to rest her tired mind—worried her fascination with death would've kept her up through the night.

It bothered him, how her thoughts went to such a dark place in the middle of the night, pressuring him to make such a promise: to detach himself from the pain of losing her, should the day ever come when she was no longer around. He understood why, having lived through the same experience back in Barstow, a similar nightmare having tormented him their entire journey to Hesperia.

Still, it bothered him. But in her current state—her eyes closed, lost in the arms of a dream—she appeared to be at peace; present but blissfully unaware.

He didn't want to spoil the moment.

Hoping to not disturb her, Havoc removed himself from last night's embrace. He felt Gillette's body stir beneath him as he started to leave, detecting his sudden withdrawal, but the joy of sleep held her eyes shut as he rolled away. And he let out a sigh of relief as she settled back into her motionless rhythm, his absence dismissed for a passing wind.

Free to roam, Havoc tip-toed over to the room's bookshelves, curious to see what the household had deemed worthy to add to their personal collection through the years. Reading the titles alone, nothing felt familiar. But as he continued to scan their paperback spines, he noticed the family had developed a taste for certain authors, owning entire bodies of work (sometimes several editions) from a select few of them. He considered the notion of such a compulsion peculiar but entertaining. And it wasn't until his second pass through that a novel's title piqued his interest, from an author he'd never come across back home.

"I see you've taken a liking to my husband's book collection," a hushed voice said.

Havoc turned to find the mother of the house had made her way into the room without making a sound—not wanting to startle her guests, should they still be asleep. She noticed Gillette's quiescent frame and sidled her way to the other side of the room to join him in front of her husband's bookcases.

"Please forgive the mess," she whispered. "Gibson has always had an affinity for such relics; literature being only one of them." She motioned to the rest of the room in one broad swoop. "For a while it felt as though a new obsession would develop every other year, but his first love has been and *always will be* music. And if you stay here long enough, he may subject you and your friend to a record or two, and the running commentary that follows after every track, sometimes lasting long after the final note of the album has faded into the æther."

"You make it sound like a punishment."

"It can feel that way sometimes, especially when he sings along."

A smile edged its way to the woman's lips, betraying any previous implication of discomfort. She tried to conceal it by clearing her throat, drawing Havoc's attention away from her husband's boxed vinyl collection and back to the bookshelves.

"But I feel it's safe to presume your interests pull you more toward the written word than anything else," she said.

"Is it that obvious?"

"My dear. If there's one thing that hasn't changed since the Fall, it's the transparency of human interest."

"What do you mean?"

The woman turned her gaze to Gillette's still slumbering frame for a second before returning it to Havoc.

"Although we'd never admit it, our curiosities tend to reveal a lot about ourselves—aspects of our personality we'd wish to keep buried. For example, your love for literature. It tells me more about you than any late-night conversation could ever uncover. For you, reading acts as a distraction from whatever thoughts might otherwise occupy your free time. It also tells me you prefer solitude above anything else, that you find solace in a silent moment." Again, her attention shifted to Gillette. "Which is why I don't buy the 'we're just friends' narrative. You don't seem the type who would devote several days on a trip with someone, even if they were a close friend; I believe your relationship with her goes beyond such innocent simplicity. As my husband has often said after he's read one of these works of fiction that rest before us: *subtext is everything*. There's an unspoken tension between the two of you, yet you both continue to deny its existence. Why?"

"We've known each other since we were kids," Havoc said.

"And that's an issue?"

"There's already so much history between us." Havoc made a quick side-glance, to see if Gillette had stirred at all, hoping to keep their conversation as private as possible. "It's not like we don't have our fair share of enjoyable memories together—because we do, don't get me wrong—but we've also shared several painful experiences and other unpleasant moments during our time growing up."

"So you've already built a strong foundation. You've been through a lot together, it seems—seen each other at your worst. I'll be honest, I'm still not seeing an issue."

"But who's to say it'll work out?"

"Ah, but that's just it. There's no guarantee that it will."

"Then why risk it?"

"It's the same reason we get out of bed every morning: to see where the day will lead us. Nothing, not even tomorrow, is promised. And I'd rather live a life worth looking back on, even one stained with regret, over having not lived at all—too afraid to take a chance. Learn to embrace the chaos, no matter the outcome."

Subtle movement from the other side of the room drew Havoc's attention away from their conversation. An older gentleman poked his head out from around the corner. The husband, he presumed.

"Aria, there you are," he said, relief in his voice. "Marshall and Laney wanted to know if they could join me out in the fields today. I figured I'd ask before I told them yes, in case you needed them around the house to help with our . . . guests."

"I'll be fine without them." She shooed him away with a wave, letting him know his presence was no longer needed. "And besides, I'm sure Willow will be more than overjoyed when she hears she's going to have the house to herself."

Her husband left without complaint, shutting the door behind him; his words muffled as he traveled down the hallway, to tell Laney and Marshall the good news.

Alone again, Aria traced back, having nearly forgotten where she left off before their interruption.

"Consider telling her how you feel," she said.

"But—"

"No. There's no 'but' to this conversation; no alternative. Consider telling her how you feel. It doesn't have to be today. It doesn't even have to be tomorrow, but don't wait until the last minute to—"

"What are you two going on about?"

Both Havoc and Aria turned to find Gillette had finally risen from her slumber, the sun in her eyes. Havoc smiled, taking in all the highlighted details that had been brought to the forefront by the sun's morning rays—how the deep shade of green in her eyes accented well against the loose strands of playful auburn that now hung beneath her tired brow, wondering how such a detail had managed to go unnoticed until today.

"Did you sleep well?" Aria asked, avoiding the question.

Gillette stretched and nodded. "I probably could've slept a while longer, had the sun not woken me."

"She'd sleep all day if she could."

"How long do you two plan on staying in town?"

"We'll be out of your hair by tomorrow morning."

"Because I spoke with my husband last night and he said he's fine with you two staying as long as you need before continuing your trip out west, so don't feel like you're being rushed to leave."

"One more night should be fine."

"So you'll be here for dinner?"

Havoc pointed to his knapsack. "You don't have to go out of your way to feed us. We have our own food."

"Canned beans?" Aria scoffed at such a concept. "I would be remiss if I allowed such an atrocity to be consumed under my roof." She wandered over to where Havoc and Gillette's knapsacks rested and carried them with her to the door. "This will ensure that you're both fed properly during your stay."

Havoc went to object but Aria held up a hand in protest.

"Do not fight me on this, my dear. I simply will not stand for it."

"Then could you at least let us remove some of our other valuables before you carry them off somewhere else?" Havoc said, his words desperate in their tone and execution.

"What do you need?"

But before Havoc could answer her, Aria opened one of the knapsacks in front of them. A look of concern overcame her as she studied the contents inside. She lifted her gaze. Her eyes bounced between her two guests, a question at the tip of her tongue.

"Is something wrong?" Gillette asked.

"Neither of you brought a change of clothes with you?"

"We didn't think we'd need to bring one," Havoc explained. "We originally planned for a weekend trip, there and back. But then we ran into a complication or two with our car and we've been making our way on foot ever since."

Aria's face lit up, an idea forming. Without speaking, she turned and disappeared into the hallway; her guests' knapsacks still in hand. Left alone in the room, Havoc and Gillette exchanged glances, both confused by such an abrupt maneuver on Aria's behalf. They shrugged in unison, hesitant, wondering if one of them should've followed her.

She returned minutes later carrying a basket of clothes, a proud smile on her face. Havoc and Gillette's bags were nowhere to be seen. She made her way to the couch and dumped the pile, humming a tune as she sorted through each layer of clothing: a pair of jeans and a gray t-shirt on one cushion; a dress, two skirts, and an array of female-designed tops on the other.

"There. I've given you both something to change into so I can wash those clothes of yours. And judging by the look of you two, you should fit comfortably in some of mine and Gibson's clothes. Please leave what you're currently wearing by the door when you're finished; I'll wash it down by the river with the rest of our laundry after breakfast." She beamed and winked as she headed for the door.

Gillette stared at her options, a puzzled and foul look on her face.

"What's the matter?" Havoc asked.

He watched as she lifted the dress from the couch to examine it further. She held the article of clothing with just the tips of her thumbs and forefingers, not wanting to acknowledge its existence any more than she had to. Her grimace expanded the more she looked at it, completely unsatisfied.

"Gill?"

"It's just so . . . bland."

"Gill."

"No, seriously, look at it. It's brown. And her tops? They're either white or gray, with nothing to help make them pop. Even the skirts come across as uninspired. There's no variation to her wardrobe whatsoever; all she owns is either brown, white, or gray. It's unappealing."

"Maybe it's all they have here. And besides, you only have to wear it while she's washing our clothes. You can go back to your denim and faded band tees first thing tomorrow."

"Fine, but I'm wearing my flannel around my waist," she huffed as she untied the aforementioned button-up from her waistline. "At least let there be some color to my outfit. Now if you would be so kind."

She motioned for him to turn around.

Havoc diverted his attention elsewhere. His eyes wandered along the perimeter of the room, hypnotized by the wealth of historical keepsakes that lined its walls, some he recognized: old, faded movie posters, some of the artwork hand drawn, their attention to detail a breathtaking accomplishment on its own; framed portraits of city landscapes, one of which caught his eye—a prewar portrait of Los Angeles, the city's skyline lit up at sunset, its streets teeming with life underneath a violet-blue sky, a full moon shining in the background — how it managed to capture the city's elegance (its golden standard) and memorialize it for the postwar generation. The image itself brought a smile to his face as he thought of their journey's approaching end: the feel of an ocean breeze against his skin, a playful wind reshaping his hair into a tousled mess as wave after wave crashed into the coastal sands of Southern California, and a family of shorebirds flew overhead while they preyed for their midday meal.

"It's strange, isn't it?"

"Hm?"

"This entire trip, us being here, and everywhere we've been since we left Paradise. It's weird, right?"

"I'm not sure I follow you."

"When we were growing up we always knew there were other cities and settlements out in the world, but we never considered them to be anything more than a passing town on our way to somewhere else. Yet here we are, in someone else's home; a place full of life, a history of its own. Before last night, we were nothing to these people — not even strangers, less than that. We didn't exist until we arrived, asking for a place to stay. And come tomorrow, after we leave, we'll become a story they tell their family and close friends: two weary travelers who spent a couple of nights in their father's study after a hellish evening in the town before theirs."

"Havoc."

"It's weird, I know. How something as simple as random objects in someone's room could evoke such a — "

"Havoc."

"What is it?" he said, his eyes still on the portrait of Los Angeles.

"You can turn around now."

His motions tentative and slow, Havoc turned. The revelation of Gillette's refashioned attire on full display, he couldn't recall how she looked before the transformation. For years she had worn nothing but denim skirts, faded band tees, and assorted flannels. But as he continued to take in her current ensemble, any memory of her past sense of style had been pushed aside. Not even the flannel around her waist or leather combat boots could trigger a visual of the outfit that had come before it. The brown dress, with one of the plain white tops underneath it, fit her well. It aged her appropriately. She no longer resembled the hardened teen-aged girl he had grown up with within the halls of a movie theater back home, but a refined young woman; her boots and flannel the only link to her past.

"Is it too much?"

He didn't have an answer for her. Instead, he continued to take it all in, admiring the way it all had somehow matured her.

"It's too much, isn't it?"

"Gill, stop it. You look great."

"Great?"

"Phenomenal, even."

Gillette looked down when she heard this—a futile attempt to hide a warm smile, her cheeks now flushed.

"You really think so?"

"C'mon now. How long have you and I known each other?" Havoc laughed. "You of all people should know I'd tell you if I thought otherwise. Trust me, the outfit suits you well."

Gillette turned her head to the other side of the couch, where the pair of jeans and gray t-shirt rested.

"Now it's your turn," she said, still smiling from Havoc's compliment, as she covered her eyes with the palms of her hands and pivoted her body to face the opposite direction.

Havoc chuckled when he noticed his scant selection. He thought it humorous, the preconceived notion that a man would never request more than one option to pick from when clothing was involved. Like any other offhand meditation he'd taken part in, Havoc wondered how far back such a convention had taken root in human development and if future generations would continue to pass the tradition forward to their children for ages to come, or if they would choose to break the cycle and allow it to be forgotten over time.

There was a knock at the door, followed by Aria's cheerful tone, wondering if the two were decent enough for her to come in. Gillette stole a quick glance at Havoc as he finished pulling his pants up, giving Aria the go-ahead to enter the room.

"Well don't you two look lovely," she said as she closed the door behind her, a leather jacket and one of their knapsacks in hand. "Gosh, talk about taking a trip down memory lane." She shook her head in disbelief. "Boy, does this send me back. It reminds me of when Gibson and I were about your age. Like you two, we grew up together. All we knew growing up was Hesperia. And like you two, the moment we were of age, we struck out on a little trip of our own to the Pacific. It really was. . . ."

Aria's voice trailed off, her eyes lost in a sea of past moments. Her gaze traded expressions, from fond remembrance to nostalgic melancholy; her memories a painful reminder that her youth was behind her. She forced a smile and pushed back a set of tears.

"You two should spend your time elsewhere, somewhere out and about while you're here for the day." Her voice cracked near the end, unable to hide her sadness. "I wouldn't want you to waste away inside our home when you could be enjoying the sunshine." She handed Gillette the knapsack and leather jacket to give to Havoc. "There's a bit of a breeze, so try and stay warm; a cold is the last thing either one of you need during your trip. How you've managed to come this far without getting one is a mystery to me. Also, I noticed a Polaroid camera in one of your bags as I removed the cans of food. Please, do yourselves a favor and take as many pictures as you can during your trip. Trust me when I say you'll regret not having something to look back on years later if you don't."

She paused for a moment, her thoughts still lost to the past.

"Well, that's enough out of me for the morning. You two enjoy your day out on the town." She closed the door behind her as she left, still wearing the same sad smile from earlier.


A SHALLOW WIND GREETED THEM as they stepped outside. The city appeared alive in the light of day. Desert sand danced in a family of small concentric circles across the entire neighborhood. The sound of wind chimes playing in imperfect harmony with one another could be heard in every direction, an occasional note out of key with their nearby counterpart. Voices of children collecting in a sea of laughter and playtime hysterics carried a weightless charm throughout the entire scene. The roaring engines of automobiles, their rumbling purr a soothing presence as they passed. It conjured memories from their childhood, when they could spend their mornings and afternoons with such reckless abandon, their impending doom only made apparent when the town's warning bell would ring at sunset

"This town is bigger than I imagined," Gillette said as she looked around, continuing to take in its many sights and sounds. "It's funny, isn't it? how much a town can appear to grow overnight."

"You could get lost in a place like this."

"If we did, we could always follow the wind chimes back home."

"Is that what we're calling this place? Home?"

"It certainly has its similarities to Paradise; you can't deny that."

He couldn't. She had him there. The scenery, while not a beat-for-beat replica of Paradise's antiquated framework, breathed an energy that could've been mistaken for it if his eyes were closed. Hesperia's visual aesthetic, however, reminded him of Ithaca: its terrain flat and open, with small patches of green grass and local wildflowers growing here and there to add a splash of color to what would've been an otherwise barren and uninspired landscape; the calming sound of the river as it flowed southwest in the distance, its existence undisturbed, and trees tall enough to climb and pretend you had left the real world behind—for a place celestial and otherworldly in nature. It all felt as if some unknown force had created the city of Hesperia with Havoc in mind, forging an amalgamation of his two childhood homes into one place; a place where all his cherished memories could live together in solemn unison.

Fragmented conversation surrounded them as they traveled north along the sidewalk, avoiding the cracks in the pavement. Everyone carried on with their day without interruption, everyone's movements perfectly orchestrated: the town a living organism. Men and women tended to their daily routines. Some were out in the fields, others headed for the river to either collect water for the house or to wash their laundry, while the rest stayed at home and looked after those too small to join the other children in the streets and lose themselves to the collective of childish wonder and imagination. And the further they traveled away from the blanket of small town suburbia the further Havoc's thoughts fell in on themselves, his emotions unpredictable in their direction.

"Are you okay?" Gillette asked. "You're looking kind of pale."

"No, I'm fine; a little homesick, if anything."

"Do you want to head back to the house?"

"Aria would just send us back out," Havoc laughed. "She'd proba-bly devise a scavenger hunt of sorts just to keep us in town until the early hours of the evening. *You can't come into the house until you've done x,y, and z,*" he said in his best impression of her.

"Why don't we?"

"A scavenger hunt?"

"Yeah, why not?"

"I was only kidding."

"Still, it sounds like it would be fun. And what better way is there to explore a new town than to try and find all the little clichés often found in places such as this?"

"Where would we even begin?"

"We're already on our way to the river. Let's start there."

"What would we be looking for?"

"I'm sure there's bound to be a tree or two nearby with someone's initials carved into them. And if not, I guess we'll just have to leave a mark of our own; a little memento for younger children to stare at and wonder what H + G could possibly mean. A cryptic message from the past by chance, its significance an unsolvable mystery."

"You've thought this through, haven't you?"

"Maybe," Gillette said.

She grabbed Havoc by the arm and led him toward the sound of the river, making their way through a small crowd of children here and there, a child asking if they would like to join them in their world of make-believe. But youthful anticipation persuaded her to continue northbound, the river's subdued song her primary focus. Having only known the view of the Nevada desert, with Havoc's tale of growing up in the lush fields of Ithaca, Nebraska being nothing more than a mental portrait, abstract and without shape or form, Gillette's curiosity knew no bounds; a humble return to such a sunny disposition.

When they finally reached the river's edge Havoc watched as his childhood friend stood and stared at the body of water, awestricken by its unwavering presence. Time ceased to exist as she took it all in. He could see it in her eyes: she wanted to know its history, its silent dialogues from centuries long since passed, all the secrets it swore to keep with every wandering soul who happened to cross its path. She wanted to take part, become another footnote in the river's earth-long catalog of clandestine exchanges.

"I can't even begin to fathom," she said. Her eyes left the inlet and met Havoc's inquisitive stare. A wave of sorrow had stained her once gentle features. "You had the privilege of knowing such beauty in your youth. And to find yourself forced to leave it all behind for something as uninspired as Paradise . . ." Her saddened gaze returned to the flow-ing body of water, still captivated by its majesty. "It must be bittersweet for you . . . to see something like this again."

Havoc let a quiet moment develop, allowing every languid motion of Mother Nature a chance to breathe a life of its own. He listened as the faint sound of birds chirping in the distance filled the air; felt the kiss of a northern wind as it roused the tree's branches to life, their leaves dancing in a foreign rhythm; watched as the women and older children of Hesperia settled into a rhythm of their own, washing and scrubbing their household's garments clean for the upcoming week.

To speak would only ruin it.

Gillette soon wandered off, her sights set on the lonesome tree that had made the riverbank its home. But Havoc stayed behind, content with the panoramic view set out before him. He observed Gillette's determination pay off as she made contact with her intended target. Her fingers grazed its wooden exterior as she circled it. Her feet disappeared beneath the waterline for a second or two as she made her way around its circumference, a euphoric expression detailing the edges of her cheeks the entire time. And when she reemerged from behind her oaken companion she motioned for Havoc to join her, insistent they share the moment.


"AS LUCK WOULD HAVE IT," Gillette said as Havoc made his final approach, "our wooden friend here has yet to be marked. And in honor of all the other marked trees around the world, I say we shouldn't let this one go overlooked a second longer."

"You're really leaning into the whole scavenger hunt idea we mentioned earlier, aren't you?"

"Only the part where we carve our initials into a tree." She reached for Havoc's firearm, holding it by the barrel to knock some of the bark loose, exposing the tree's softer interior. "Not even you can deny the pull such an impulse can have to leave something, a small piece of yourself, behind for others to stumble upon and admire long after we're gone; eager to know what hidden meaning might lie underneath its surface, if anything at all."

"I guess there's no stopping you, is there?"

"What's done is done."

The sentiment tickled Havoc's insides. It relieved him from last night's conversation to see his friend enjoying herself again, even if it meant watching her do something as infantile as carving two letters into an old oak tree. But the act itself, while juvenile in its technique, left him curious. With everything left behind to remember the past by previous generations—some having lasted centuries after their humble creation—he wondered if humanity's relevance had come to an end, any prospect of experiencing a return to form gone. Their time on earth would amount to nothing, every precious moment rendered insignificant in an instant. But hope replaced any doubt he may have felt when he witnessed the smile of accomplishment work its way to Gillette's cheeks, admiring her handiwork: a jagged H + G now for ever a part of the tree's identity.

"Y'know," Havoc said as he pulled the camera from his knapsack to take a quick snapshot. "If the mysticism behind this tree's newfound marking is to gain any traction, we may have to find our way back here to help perpetuate the myth."

"Come back to Hesperia?"

"Why not? After all, it's as you said—this place does share a lot of similarities with Paradise. And if for some reason we find out we can't make it back home, this place could work as a substitute."

Gillette looked around, taking in the city of Hesperia as a whole, silently appraising everything it had to offer.

"It'll never replace the comfort I felt back home, nor does it hold a candle to Vienna's unmatched beauty." She paused to return her gaze to the oak tree, still proud of her inscription. "But I can't deny that it certainly has its charm."

# §4

## HARMONY IN ROTATION

**TIME ESCAPED THEM** as they continued to explore the town, an unexpected marvel around every corner to steal their attention; any small detail that reminded them of Ithaca or Paradise enough to carry them away in a sea of memories. Everything about Hesperia felt like a dream, almost too good to be true. It wasn't until they noticed the apparent shift in the sky's complexion, the sun on its slow descent behind the mountains, that the thought of making their way back to Aria and Gibson's crossed their minds. And while the absence of a warning bell confounded them, they didn't miss its odious presence—the anxiety it caused with each subsequent toll.

"Do we really have to leave tomorrow?" Gillette asked as they followed the main road. "It feels as though we've barely scratched the surface of this place. Who knows what other secrets this town has that have yet to be discovered. Surely Los Angeles can wait another day or two. It's not like it's going anywhere."

Havoc couldn't help but laugh.

"What's so funny?"

"You," he said, still amused by her behavior.

"I'm serious. We should stay another day or two so we can explore further; see what other hidden gems we can stumble across."

"We can't."

"Why not?"

"We don't want to overstay our welcome."

Havoc could tell it pained Gillette to agree with him, but knew he had a point not even she could argue against. If they were to find their way back after their visit to the coast, it would work in their favor to not wear out the city's hospitality so soon. But even as the light from the sun faded into the early hours of twilight, leading everyone inside for the evening, Havoc watched as Gillette's thoughts continued to follow a daydream; how her eyes would wander to a house where the windows remained unlit, its lifeless interior desperate and waiting to be made a home; its sense of purpose restored. Whenever this happened Gillette's hand would find Havoc's arm, a breath of excitement in her eyes as she brought the vacant residence to his attention, each one full of promise and possibility. And were it not for the approaching darkness of the coming evening he felt she would've made several attempts to drag him inside one of them: live out the fantasy of owning a home, an actual house instead of a movie theater; a first for her.

"You really like it here?" he asked.

"From everything I've seen so far, I do. I really do."


A GENTLE BREEZE CAME IN FROM THE NORTH, rousing the neighborhood's diverse family of wind chimes from their slumber so they could sing the rest of the way back. Their distant notes punctuated every step in a syncopated rhythm. And from several houses on the block, the scent of meat cooking drifted through the air. But as Aria and Gibson's home came into view, a familiar melody cut through the chorus of singing metal. It caught Havoc's ear by surprise. It was the sound of a woman's voice chanting something similar to the tune his mother used to hum throughout the day when he was a small child.

In a fit of morbid curiosity, he quickened his pace toward the front door, his mind eager to ask how the person knew such a melodic phrase. And as Havoc stepped through the door's threshold—the tune's chordal sequence no longer in question—he turned to find Aria standing in the kitchen, finishing the final touches for the family's evening meal.

She stopped the moment she saw them from the corner of her eye, a curt smile at the corner of her lips.

"I was beginning to wonder if you were going to make it back in time for dinner," she said. "Even Gibson's voiced his concerns a couple of times tonight, and he doesn't even do that with the children whenever they decide to stay out past sunset."

"That melody you were humming."

"Oh, could you hear me from outside? How embarrassing."

"How do you know it?"

"How do I know it?" Aria said, confused.

"It's something my mother used to hum all the time when I was a child. I didn't think anyone else knew it. Where did you learn it?"

"You're bound to memorize a song or two's melody living in this house. Gibson has his evenings, especially after a hard day out in the fields, where he'll listen to a handful or albums before joining the rest of the family. He says it takes him back—to what, I'll never know; I've never bothered to ask. But if it helps to keep peace within our four walls, I'm not one to judge his methods."

"Whatever you've made for dinner smells amazing," Gillette said.

Aria curtsied at such a compliment. "This year's harvest proved itself rather fruitful, and it felt fitting to make a household favorite while we have guests. Other than the occasional family member or childhood friend, we hardly ever have company over. While unexpected, we consider your presence here an absolute treat."

"Does it have a name?"

"I'm sure it did at some point or another," Aria said as she carried the plate to the dining room. "It's probably some fancy, unpronounceable name from somewhere faraway, but we've just come to call it vegetable stew around here. While we tend to keep with the old traditions from before the Fall, remembering what to call a prepared dish felt pointless in the grand scheme of things; wouldn't you agree?"

"As long as it tastes good," Gibson's voice joined the conversation as he carried a silver platter of grilled chicken in from outside, "I don't care in the slightest what it's called. And if it manages to leave my stomach feeling full at the end of it, all the better."

Gibson placed the flatware at the center of the table, next to Aria's stirred vegetables, and greeted his wife with a small kiss on the cheek before calling for the children to join them in the dining room, warning them that there may not be any left in the next couple of minutes. He winked at Havoc and Gillette, a silent tell to his kidding nature.

Once everyone had gathered around the table, with everything in place and ready to be eaten, picture perfect and pristine, Havoc's thoughts drifted to Macro—how he would've spent several hours trying to capture the ambiance of the scene before him on film. His eyes met Gillette's as she sat across from him. He could tell her mind had wandered to the same place, remembering the first person to take them in on their trip in a rather fond light. He found it hard to believe that only three days had passed since they left him behind to continue their journey toward the coast. He wondered if Macro had taken up on Gillette's offer to head east for Paradise. And if he did, Havoc hoped he made it there okay.

He tried hard not to think of Allele and Vector, or of Barstow all together. The haunting images of his time there didn't need another second of consideration. He wanted to bury the memory of that night, to forget it ever happened. Because while it pained him to betray one of Allele's final words of sentiment, to not let the citizens of Barstow be forgotten . . . the emotional toll it would cost him to remember their sacrifice would've been too much for him to bear.

"Aria was telling me you have a penchant for literature," Gibson said between bites.

"And a history with music, it seems," Aria interjected. "He was just telling me his mother used to hum a tune when he was a child. And as it turns out, the song just happens to be from one of those records you listen to before dinnertime."

"Is that so?" Gibson said, a faint glimmer in his eye. "Perhaps we'll have to figure out which song it is once we're done eating. We can make an evening of it before we turn in for the night."

"It's one of those piano-heavy tracks from that redheaded woman you enjoy listening to every now and then, the one with the spaghetti Western style whistle if I'm remembering it correctly—to save you the trouble of spending all night looking for it." Aria smiled and winked, letting Havoc know she had spared him from listening to Gibson's entire record collection.


THEY SPENT THE REST OF THEIR TIME around the dinner table lost in aimless discussion and laughter. A carefree energy emanated throughout the evening: a story from Gibson and Aria's youth would pop up on occasion despite endless protest from the children, having heard them a thousand times before. The concept of eating a meal together as a family an experience unlike any other, Havoc thought such a tradition only existed in the world of pure fiction. And it wasn't until the children asked to be excused that the conversation left the comfort of the dining room, with Gibson leading Havoc into his study as Aria asked Gillette if she would like to help clear the table, eager to hear if she and Havoc enjoyed their day out on the town.

"How long have you two known each other?" Gibson asked as he took a seat in his recliner and pulled a box of records from the shelf next to him. "A long time, I presume?"

"Ever since we were six years old, so just shy of seventeen years."

"That's a long time, more than half your life."

"Yeah, tell me about it. There are moments where she'll bleed into past memories from before I knew her. And even after my brain corrects itself—that she couldn't possibly have been there with me in the fields of Nebraska—a small part of her will remain a couple seconds longer before she fades away entirely."

"Memories have a way of betraying us like that," Gibson said, his attention still lost in the mess of vinyl. "My children are the perfect example of such a phenomenon. They may have only been on this earth for a brief time, but I sometimes have trouble remembering my life without them. It's as if they've always been there in the background, even if the truth would argue otherwise. You'd swear the brain was trying to rewrite its own history. Ah, here we are! Finally, the one we've been looking for."

His motions fluid in their execution, Gibson removed the vinyl from its sleeve and carried it to the other side of the room where his record player rested. It all appeared effortless: the way he prepared the black disc, laying it where it belonged, moved the needle to its proper place and lowered it with such surgical precision; watched as it fell into a groove and let the speakers come to life; listened as the haunting presence of a female's vocals and processed drums bled into the æther and consumed the room. Havoc felt the room's entire mood change, observed as Gibson closed his eyes fell into the thick of it, and acknowledged that something transformative had taken place in front of him; something sublime and sacred.

One could get lost in the warmth of its hypnotic spell.

"So," Gibson said, his eyes still closed. "Aria pointed out that your mother used to sing when you were a child. I take it music was important in your family while growing up?"

"My mother died when I was real little, my father joining her a few years after. The only music I'd been exposed to at that point was the little number she would hum in the evening while she made supper, the same number Aria was humming earlier tonight as Gillette and I walked through the front door."

"How funny that it happened to be the same tune your mother knew. What are the odds of that? It's why I asked if music had been important in your family. It's not often that two people and from different parts of the country by the sound of things—will manage to replicate the same melody note-for-note unless they were both exposed to the same stimuli. And the fact it—"

Gibson cut himself short as the second track started. He pointed at the record player with untethered excitement. Havoc listened as the song's opening instrumentation left the stereo: mandolin and drums set the stage for bass and piano to make their grand entrance, followed by the soul-stirring spaghetti Western whistle Aria had mentioned earlier. But when the vocal melody started, Havoc froze. His mind reeled back to when he was a small boy, memories of his mother's silhouette floating across the kitchen floor as she lost herself to the motions of preparing the day's evening meal. For a brief moment the decorated walls of Gibson's study faded into the backdrop and allowed the recollection some time to shine at the forefront of his current surroundings. Meanwhile, tears of fond reminiscence threatened to fall as the song continued to play.

"I know that look," Gibson said.

Havoc slipped back to reality. The room reverted back to its organized mess of prewar memorabilia; the memory of his mother no longer present, but a distant dream.

"Hm?"

"That look," Gibson continued. "I've seen it before on my wife and children whenever they happened to stumble into my study while I'm in one of my listening moods after work. It's the look of nostalgia; an unexplained sensation. It'll often leave you feeling confused as to how something from before your time could have such an emotional impact on you. But somehow it manages to lift us from our current state and throws us into a place that shouldn't feel familiar, yet we can't help but get lost in the moment. We welcome it and pray the feeling never goes away. And when the final song of the album comes to a close, we find ourselves back here in the present, where we belong, to continue living out our lives until we can find the time to come back to it and escape for another hour or two."

Unspoken inspiration pulled Gibson from the comfort of his chair and back to the other side of the room. He removed another box from the shelf, this one smaller than the first, and sorted through it for a couple of minutes. He retrieved a handful of compact, rectangular cartridges to bring back with him and held them in front of his guest.

"Here. You should take these with you when you and Gillette leave tomorrow. That way you two will have something to listen to for the rest of your trip."

"What are they?" Havoc said.

"They're cassette tapes: music made portable. All you have to do is put this small cartridge in your stereo cassette drive that's in the car's dashboard and turn the volume up so you can to listen to an entire album from front to back."

"Gillette and I would love that. But unfortunately we've been without a vehicle since the first leg of our journey."

"You've made it all the way here from Nevada on foot?"

"Yeah."

"Take my car," Gibson said.

"What?"

"Take my car. I can always hitch a ride to the fields with one of the neighbors. I'd rather you and Gillette not push yourselves to complete exhaustion just to see the Pacific. You'd spend the majority of your time there resting, and I'd rather you two be allowed to enjoy yourselves while you're there."

"We couldn't."

"Nonsense. I'll give you a few cans of peanut oil to take you to Los Angeles and back. You can always return the car when you're finished with it. Now please, take these cassettes and accept the offer. I won't take no for an answer."

The door opened before Havoc could respond. Gillette and Aria's warm smiles entered the room, both laughing quietly to themselves as they closed the door behind them. Gibson looked outside to find the rest of the neighborhood had gone dark.

"Is it time for bed already?"

"That it is, my dear," Aria said, still beaming. "And don't sound surprised. We both know you've been prone to lose track of time when you come in here to listen to one of your records."

Gibson held his hands up in defeat. He turned to Havoc and extended his right arm. "I guess this is where tonight's introduction into the world of music shall come to a close," he said. "Goodnight you two. We shall reconvene first thing in the morning."

Aria laughed at her husband's departing sentiment and led him into the hallway and out of sight, letting the door close behind them.

"He's a little weird," Gillette said.

"Yeah, he's kind of an oddball." Havoc looked down at the four cassette tapes he'd been given, one of them being the same album he'd listened to earlier, still processing the night's events. "But you get used to it after a while."

"What are those?'

"Music to play in the car during the rest of our trip."

"The car?"

"Gibson offered us his vehicle to finish the final leg of our trip; said he wouldn't take no for an answer. He even offered to let us use some of his peanut oil instead of our own."

"That was sweet of him."

"Yeah, I'm still trying to understand it myself."

His attention returned to the four small cartridges that rested in his hand, unable to comprehend such a kind gesture from someone who had been a stranger a day go.

WITH THE LIGHTS OUT, the moon's radiance the only thing keeping the room from total darkness, Havoc sought comfort on his makeshift bedding. He tossed and turned, but sleep escaped him. His thoughts eventually returned to what Aria had said earlier that morning. He wrestled with them, weighing every outcome if he decided to tell Gillette the truth. And with every counter-argument Aria's voice continued to echo: *Consider telling her how you feel. Embrace the chaos, no matter the outcome.*

But he couldn't do it. Whenever he looked up at Gillette's dormant outline, he talked himself out of a confession. After years of separation, he had his friend back. He didn't want to risk losing their renewed connection over such an embarrassing revelation.

"Havoc," Gillette said as she turned to face him. "Can I ask you something?"

"Of course. What is it?"

"Is it all right if I join you again tonight?"

"Gill, you never have to ask such a question. I mean, we've known each other most of our lives. You should know by now, you're always more than welcome to join me here on the floor, especially if you find yourself becoming preoccupied with thoughts similar to the ones you had last night."

"It's nothing like that," Gillette said as she climbed down from the couch and made herself comfortable. "I just really enjoyed our time together today, and it would feel wrong to end the day apart from one another. It sounds weird, I know, but this afternoon reminded me how much I actually missed you after you moved to the outskirts of town. I missed having you around all the time. Today felt like old times, back when we were kids."

Gillette's words stayed with Havoc the rest of the night. But even as his eyes grew heavy, Aria's remark fought to remain a hidden feature in the back of his skull. He couldn't shake their weight, not even in the comfort of his dreams.

*I'll tell her someday,* he reasoned with the voice as he closed his eyes for the evening. *It doesn't have to be today It doesn't even have to be tomorrow, but I promise I won't wait until it's too late. I'll embrace the chaos, no matter the outcome.*

# CHAPTER 5

## IN VIEW OF A ONCE BURNING CITY

# §1

---

# BEYOND THE HORIZON

THIS WAS IT, Havoc thought. The final leg of the journey. In a couple of hours he and Gillette would soon find themselves enjoying the fabled brilliance of California's southern coastline. He remained motionless on the floor, still holding Gillette as he watched the early morning sky come to life as the sun rose from its eastern slumber. The sound of automotive repair could be heard, an expletive finding its way into the air here and there, followed shortly after by a voice colored with disappointment, telling the other to watch their language around the children; a humble apology issued every time.

Mixed emotions. Something Havoc didn't expect to feel. He lifted himself from his naiant state and looked around, taking in the ambiance his makeshift bedroom had to offer one last time. Such a strange notion, he thought—how the surrounding environment could feel like home the way it did: the family library a quiet callback to the bookstore in Paradise; the wealth of movie posters all along the walls reminding him of all the hours he and Gillette spent lost in the glow of the silver screen; Gibson and Aria working on the car out front while the kids watched with intrigue, a modest recreation of the afternoons he and Gillette spent watching Ford maintain one of the many vehicles that had staggered into his shop on any given day. And then there were all the other details that reminded him of his life before Paradise: the river and the oak tree calling him back to his earliest memories of childhood with thoughts of escape and wonder; the well-oiled routine of men and women tending to their responsibilities from the break of dawn until suppertime; the smell of wildflowers lost in a summer breeze.

A part of him didn't want to leave.

"Do you think they can get any louder?" Gillette said, her eyes still closed. And as reluctant as ever to open them, she turned her attention to the window to find the colors of the morning sky had yet to settle into a comfortable shade of cerulean. "And why does nobody here appear to enjoy sleep?"

"They can't afford to living in a place like this, where there's always something to tend to or look after. If it's not the weather, it's the hours left in the day to get it all done. Time is always against them. Sleeping in could spell death for them if they were to fall too far behind."

Gillette's composure sank when she considered this, the stark contrast between her carefree lifestyle back home and the backbreaking routine-filled days the people of Hesperia were forced to endure. It humbled her to realize how fortunate of an upbringing she had been given in comparison, and to wonder if Havoc would've found himself in a similar position as an adult today had his little town of Ithaca not been met with such a terrible fate.

But that was all behind him now.

The roar of the car's engine coming to life outside their window startled them, its idling presence a reminder that their time in Hesperia would be coming to an end soon. They sighed in plaintive unison while they gathered what belongings they had before saying goodbye to the room of trinkets and other paraphernalia, with everything Gibson had salvaged from an all-but-forgotten past and restored throughout the years; a place that had served as a safe haven during their stay. This was it, Havoc's mind repeated as he and Gillette made their way down the corridor: a seventeen-year-old promise would finally be fulfilled and a young girl's dream would soon become reality.

And soon it would all be over.

Gillette paused at the end of the hallway, her attention stolen by a small credenza occupied by a family of framed photographs, most of them candid snapshots of the three children running around outside while others documented moments of life inside their home; their narrative remained a mystery. But the one her eyes always came back to was a picture of Aria and Gibson when they were younger, about the same age she and Havoc were now, standing in front of the place they called home; warm smiles on both of their faces while locked in a loving embrace, their happiness on full display.

Havoc could tell it made her miss her mother and father.

"Do you think we'll ever have what they have?" she said. "What mine and your parents had."

"It's possible." Havoc laid a hand on her shoulder. "There's no promise it'll be easy, that it won't be hard work, but it's possible."

"It's weird. While growing up, thoughts of adulthood—getting a place of my own, falling in love, starting a family, watching my children grow up, growing old—never crossed my mind. But being here with Aria and Gibson and their kids, seeing these photographs, knowing their lives will continue to unfold long after we're gone . . . it's led my mind to wander and daydream of one day sharing moments similar to theirs, but with a family of my own."

She paused and let her thoughts hang in the air. Her gaze left the arrangement of photographs and fell to her shoulder, Havoc's hand still there for comfort. A faint smirk slipped across her face upon seeing it. Her hand found its way to where his rested and met it with its own breath of confidence.

"Not for some time, of course," she said. "But seeing their life story romanticized in such a fashion; it's enough to make me want it at some point in the future."

"Ah, there you are!" Aria's voice bounced with glee as she stepped into the foyer through the screen door. "I was about to come in and wake you two so you could join us out front. Gibson's been getting the car ready for you to take to the coast."

"Oh, we could hear him," Gillette said.

"I hope we didn't wake you with all the commotion."

"Havoc was already awake and getting ready as he usually is before the break of dawn, but it did rouse me from a rather pleasant dream."

Aria turned toward Havoc. "An early bird, I take it?"

"Yeah. You can blame my father for that," Havoc said. "While we were heading west from Nebraska when I was a child he would wake me as the color in the sky started to shift from its twilit shade of midnight blue and come to life. The tradition of doing so has stuck with me ever since, even years after his passing. It's become a part of who I am, to sit and watch the start of a new day unfold before me first thing in the morning—a myriad of possibilities resting on the horizon."

He turned his attention to the table of photographed memories. A daydream of his own stirred from within. A brief flicker.

"And who knows. Perhaps I'll pass the custom to a child of my own someday; let it live on through them."


DISBELIEF MET GILLETTE when they stepped outside and saw the vehicle with her own eyes, finding it hard to believe that something so small and unassuming could be capable of such an uproar. But Havoc could tell by the car's angular framework, its compact design, it had been built for speed, and that Gibson had modified it with a bigger engine in his spare time to better suit his needs when it came to working in the fields.

"Look who decided to join the land of the living," Aria said as they approached the vehicle's passenger side window.

"Are you sure we can't go with them?" Willow asked her mother, projecting her lower lip in a stern-faced pout. "We could show them all the best spots to visit, and which ones to avoid."

"I don't think they'd appreciate three stowaways tagging along on their trip to see the coast."

The youngest of the three continued to make her case; resilient, as little ones usually were at her age. She tried to reason with them from every possible angle she could imagine, but her parents shot her down without hesitation. Not even the prospect of the house being kid-free for a few days could convince them to agree to such an arrangement. Havoc laughed, finding Willow's determination to break her parents down one argument after another respectable--that once she set her mind on a goal, she refused to let it go without giving it everything she had. And even when she finally accepted defeat, the small child didn't go quietly.

"She gets her stubbornness from you, you know," Aria said as Gibson finished getting the car ready.

"Yes, and she gets her ability to forge such an elaborate argument out of thin air from you. She is our daughter, after all."

"The best of both of us."

"And the worst," Gibson said with a sly grin.

He circled the vehicle twice, making sure everything was in working order. And when he finally considered himself satisfied with his handiwork, he slapped the hood of the car before stepping away to admire it further. The entire process sent Havoc back to a memory of his father during their time on the road, always fine-tuning the car's diesel engine and checking the tire pressure first thing in the morning before they left to continue their journey along the Interstate.

"She's all yours and ready to go," Gibson said.

"I promise we won't be gone too long," Havoc promised. "We'll be back before you have a chance to miss her."

"Just bring her back in one piece is all I ask."

Gillette made the first move, opening the passenger side door to slide onto its worn leather seat. Havoc followed her lead, finding his place behind the wheel. Comfort found his fingertips as they glided across the dash. And while the feel of its wooden finish didn't carry the same sentimental value as his father's, the subtle caress of flesh against machine (of organic against the artificial) still carried his mind elsewhere as he felt the engine rumble underneath. It allowed him a minute or two to collect himself and reorganize his thoughts before setting out on the open road ahead.

"It feels weird, being in a car again," Gillette said as she buckled herself in. "While I'm excited to see Los Angeles a lot sooner than if we had continued on foot, I'd be lying if I said I wasn't going to miss our daylong excursions along the highway."

Havoc laughed as he shifted the vehicle into gear, finding her remark worthy of a brief snigger. Their walk from Barstow to Hesperia set aside from the rest, he agreed with the sentiment. Had it not been for the unfortunate blowout at the beginning of their trip, they wouldn't have had all this time to truly reconnect: a blessing in disguise. Because without it they would've made it to the coast and back by now, Gillette having returned to her daily routine of preparing film after film to watch on one of the theater's still functioning projectors; and Havoc would've found himself back to living on the outskirts of town, enjoying his weekly read in complete solitude.

And as they made their way to the Interstate, the sun now well overhead, Havoc fought to not look back in his rear-view mirror; afraid if he did he would feel the same energy he had the day his father collected him from his room and drove away from his first childhood home—that he would watch the town of Hesperia disappear forever in a cloud of dust the same way Paradise had at the beginning of his and Gillette's westbound travels. Instead, he focused on the vast mountain range ahead of him. Its jagged peaks continued to reach for the heavens above. An everlasting exercise in futility. Vacant remains of an old communication tower could be seen in the distance: unoccupied and without power, any sense of purpose it may have had lost to the past; its existence rendered insignificant the day the world thought it was coming to an abrupt end.

He wondered if anyone had ever made it to the top.

# §2

# BECOMING SILHOUETTES

IT WASN'T UNTIL THEY reached the other side of the mountain range when the scenery changed. The timeworn details of desert sand, ossified cacti and Joshua trees, and the occasional road sign fell to the wayside, replaced by war-torn skyscrapers and a sea of faceless billboards. Rusted remnants of automobiles lined both sides of the city's many streets as Havoc continued to cruise down the middle of the Interstate. He knew he shouldn't have expected to see the same vibrant view he had witnessed in Gibson's study, that Los Angeles would be a hollowed spectre of its former self, but he couldn't shake the inerrant beauty of the photograph from his memory. Where unrivaled grandeur once stood, desolation greeted him.

Everything lay in ruin.

"Stop the car," Gillette said.

"Why? Is something wrong?"

"Not at all," she said. She reached for one of their bags in search of the Polaroid camera. "I just would like to take a picture or two of the city while we still have the chance to do so; capture its beauty before we become one with it."

Havoc watched as Gillette readied the camera to take aim at the city before her. Her breathing slowed. She measured every inhale and exhale. Took her time. Waited for the perfect moment before she finally pressed the shutter-release button and became mesmerized by the film's gradual development; marveled as its opaque surface surrendered itself to the captured image underneath; the expression on her face a familiar one to Havoc's eyes. It was the same look of wonderment she would often wear whenever she sat and watched a movie come to life on the silver screen. But a new element presented itself as she continued to stare at the photograph: an intimation of pride. Macro would've been proud to see his donated knickknack being put to good use, that he and Gillette had learned to take pause and appreciate the beauty of a moment and become one with time.

"I can't believe it," Gillette said, still admiring the printed image that rested in her hands, comparing it with the scenery ahead. "Los Angeles. . . . We're almost there."

"Let's just hope it was all worth the trouble."

"How could it not? Even if its days of creating Hollywood magic are behind it, we still have its history of cinema to hold us over. There is bound to be a library where reels of tape are kept in secret, waiting to be viewed by an audience. And if that ends up not being enough to satisfy our curiosities, there's always the ocean and visiting the Pier the kids mentioned."

Havoc's attention returned to the road. The midday sun hung overhead as he weighed their options. Visiting the coastline could wait, he thought. Unlike the city of Los Angeles, its monolithic architecture a recent addition to the Earth's landscape, the Pacific Ocean had been a part of the world's history from the very beginning—its ebb and flow a permanent fixture as opposed to Los Angeles' short-lived (and slowly deteriorating) existence.

"Prepare yourself," he said. He floored the gas pedal and continued down the arterial roadway toward the heart of the city.

With their windows rolled halfway, the wind in their hair, Havoc and Gillette held their breath with cautious optimism as they watched the sky move sideways. Their usual view of desert flatland having been overcome by town homes and high-rises, the sun's warm brilliance now lay hidden behind their towering presence; the road cast in an ominous shadow. Everywhere they looked, at every passing intersection, something new and exciting jumped out at them. Where the average small town lived in humble modesty, the city of Los Angeles had no issue flaunting its exuberance at every corner. But it surprised them to find its many streets and alleyways appeared vacant; not a soul or distant outcry could be seen or heard as they continued to explore their newfound surroundings.

"It's strange," Havoc said. "You'd think such a city would be teeming with life, but it's completely empty."

"It's almost as if we're the only one's here."

"This isn't how I imagined it growing up. Even with the Fall of the Atom taken into consideration, I always pictured this place as a beacon of prosperity—where people from all around traveled hundreds or thousands of miles to start anew—but it's nothing more than a ghost town; beautiful in its design but lacking in anything to make it feel even remotely human. It almost feels alien to me, these colossal structures being a monument to something completely foreign from the rest of mankind."

Gillette rolled her window the rest of the way and unbuckled her seat belt. She lifted herself through the open window frame and sat on the edge, letting the wind lift her hair in the passing breeze. Feeling nervous, Havoc removed his foot from the gas pedal and let the vehicle coast to a slower speed. He couldn't see the upper half of Gillette's body, but assumed her lips wore a tender smile from ear to ear. And from within the safety of the cab Havoc heard Gillette let out a cheerful scream into the heart of the city, letting the entire world know they had finally made it.

LOST IN THE LABYRINTH that had once been the city's downtown area, its proud epicenter, Havoc studied every street and avenue hoping to find something familiar, a landmark universal to the human experience: a movie theater to come back to after sunset. Because after all the time they'd spent on the road, he wanted to treat Gillette to a place that felt like home to end the day. He refused to settle for anything less. She deserved the comfort of falling asleep in an old projection booth overlooking the cold vacancy of a dust-covered auditorium, something to remind her of all the sleepless nights they had spent together as kids; a pleasant and reassuring reprieve after everything they had been through in the past week.

It didn't take long to find one. Its square-faced marquee an obvious betrayal to what would've been an otherwise flawless camouflage, disguising itself among all the other nondescript buildings that made up the entire district. Overcome with joy, he pulled to the side of the road as close as he could manage and shut the car's engine off before Gillette could protest to his casual parking job. But words escaped her when she saw the movie theater's signboard a couple of car links down the street from where they parked. Welcomed surprise claimed every fiber of her being.

"Just when I thought I was never going to see another theater marquee in my lifetime," she said.

"I figured we would need a place to rest for the evening come sundown." Havoc opened his car door and motioned for Gillette to follow him. "And if we were able to find such a place, which I knew we would, we should take advantage and settle down somewhere that'll remind us of Paradise as much as possible. And what better place than a multiplex in the heart of Los Angeles?"

"You have me there," Gillette said with a snide smirk. "But if I'm being honest, you didn't need to sell me on staying the night in a cineplex. I've missed the comfort of falling asleep in my own room since we left. The closest we've come to having a decent night's rest was in Gibson's study, but it still wasn't the same. But to fall asleep amongst the comfort of a projector and the undying glow of its light hitting the silver screen will always create a wave of euphoria. Its presence means everything to me, and nothing could ever replace it."

They remained silent the rest of the way as they ambled toward the theater's double-front doorway, surprised to find them unlocked. Once inside they stopped dead in their tracks—the building's interior layout identical to the one back home. Everything was where it was supposed to be. The popcorn machine lay dormant and untouched, how it operated still a mystery to them both. Layers of dust covered the support beams overhead. Undisturbed silence echoed through every corridor, hoping Havoc and Gillette's sudden arrival would break it and breathe new life into its forsaken existence.

Their curiosity carried them deeper into the lobby, up the small incline and into the hall of auditoriums. It continued to amaze them, how the theater's floor plan closely resembled their own. And were it not for the difference in carpet, they would've assumed they had been transported back to the sandy terrain of Paradise, Nevada—their entire trip to the City of Angels reduced to nothing more than a lurid fever dream; still sound asleep in Gillette's bedroom. Havoc noticed a small sensation skip across his fingertips as he felt Gillette take his hand in hers. He turned his attention away from the haunting details of the multiplex to find a playful sparkle in her eyes.

"Shall we see what's playing?" she said.

But before he had a chance to answer her, Gillette led the way down the empty hallway. Her calculated gaze shifted back and forth in quick succession, determined. She knew what she was looking for and refused to stop until she found it. It wasn't until they reached the end of the corridor that they finally stumbled upon what Gillette had been looking for: the steel door which led upstairs into the projection rooms above—the words EMPLOYEES ONLY barely visible across the top; its letters having faded over time.

"Do you think anyone's been in here since the world ended?"

"I doubt it," Havoc said. "The place looks like it hasn't seen any sign of human interaction in ages. I'd be surprised if any of the equipment still worked if I'm being honest."

"But imagine if someone had." She opened the steel door and led them into the theater's stairwell. "Do you think they would've spent the same amount of time we did growing up watching film after film, appreciating every coherent second that still remained as it made its way onto the screen? Which ones were their favorites? And did they have someone to share the experience with or were they alone? How long did they stay before deciding to abandon such a place for something beyond the horizon? Imagine if we stumbled upon a bookshop somewhere around here! Perhaps there's a small one just around the corner like back home. You could make your way through every aisle, thumb your way through every shelf, and decide to pick up some of your favorites to take with you when we head back and start a collection like Gibson has in his study."

They made their way to the storage room, where the theater's reels of tape were kept while not in use—its shelves packed from top to bottom with tin film canisters stacked neatly across the board, every row of containers waiting patiently to be removed and consumed by a faithful and eager audience. And having shown no indication of prior use, covered in its own layer of dust, Havoc wondered if the condition of each motion picture that rested before them had remained intact through the years. It thrilled him to imagine the possibility of watching some of their childhood favorites and not have to worry about the integrity of the film's composition, to be able to enjoy every minute of it frame-by-frame without interruption.

"It's a shame mother isn't here to keep the projector running while we watch something," Gillette said as she scanned every shelf. "One of us will have to stay up here to switch out the reels while the other enjoys it comfortably in the auditorium."

Havoc stepped forward and ran his fingers across the tops of a row of canisters. Underneath the thin veil of dust he could read the abbreviated title and its runtime on the title card: B.S. - 101mins. He smiled and started to remove its five corresponding containers from their resting place, making sure to keep them in the correct order as he carried them to the nearest projection booth and laid them on the chair next to the film equipment.

"You're wanted in theater four," he said with a wink as he passed Gillette on his final trip from the storage closet.

It had been years since he had operated a film projector, but still remembered the process. He made his way to the platter to set up the first reel, locking the tape into place before feeding it through the projector's many mechanisms. The entire procedure took some time, but it still fascinated him how something as brilliant and moving as a motion picture could exist in such a small and unassuming way: several thousand feet of still-framed images existing on celluloid, the film's beauty of movement and sound a well-kept secret to anyone unfamiliar with the medium. It saddened him to think there were people out there, people like Macro, who had never experienced or been exposed to the art of cinema—had never sat and watched and listened as a movie came to life on screen while they sat in an auditorium ruled by darkness. The sound of the projector above their heads as it worked diligently to keep the narrative moving forward.

He feared the day it would eventually be forgotten.

The universal hum.

From the comfort of the booth, Havoc watched the movie unfold through the small window that led into the theater. It surprised him to witness the opening scene play without issue: a married couple (middle-aged) can be seen holding an argument in a foreign tongue on a moving train, sitting across the way from the female lead while she tries to read. Their contentious conversation eventually forces her to find solace elsewhere, at the other end of the compartment; her new seat across the aisle from her male counterpart, also reading a novel. They exchange glances for only a couple of seconds as the arguing couple leaves for a moment to settle things in private, but by then it's already over for them. Before they've even spoken a word to each other, a spark has developed; hero and heroine, their destinies becoming more and more intertwined throughout the night as they wander about the streets of Vienna.

And as the movie continued to play without interruption, Havoc's gazed fell and landed on Gillette—her lone silhouette the only other human element in the room. He could only imagine the breath of emotions she must've been feeling in that moment as her favorite film danced across the screen. And if it hadn't been for the cue marks in the upper right-hand corner telling him to load the next reel of tape, he could have watched her forever.

"YOU CAN'T BE SERIOUS. What do you mean you don't want to watch your shoot 'em up movie?" Gillette said.

"It can wait."

"But it's tradition. We've always watched our favorites one after the other. Aren't you the least bit curious, the kind of experience you'll have being able to watch your favorite film from beginning to end without any disruptions? I swear, it'll feel like you're watching a completely different movie."

"Gill."

"Havoc."

"It can wait."

"But—"

"Gill . . . It can wait," he said. "There's always tomorrow for such things, and I'd much rather spend the rest of our day—with what little daylight we have left—enjoying the sandy beaches of the Pacific. After all, Gibson gave us enough peanut oil, not to mention the few cans we brought with us, to last a couple of days. We can afford to break away from our childhood tradition and embark on an adventure for a change. If we were going to waste all of our time in Los Angeles watching hours upon hours of cinematic prowess, we could've just stayed home and accomplished the exact same thing. Now let's go. The day only continues to escape us."

A sigh of defeat left Gillette's lips before she went silent. She hated to admit it, but he was right. While the idea of breaking away from their routine bothered her to no end, it would've been a disservice to the spirit of the trip, especially if she considered all the trouble they had gone through to get where they are. Reluctantly, she nodded in agreement to Havoc's suggestion. She took him by the hand and led them back downstairs and out the front door.

"Keep in mind," she said. "I may have agreed to this little side-venture of yours, but you owe me a double-feature."

"You won't have to remind me," Havoc laughed. "The look in your eyes alone will be enough."

"I'm not kidding. You owe me."

"How's this," he said. "The moment we get back to Hesperia, we'll make a day of it. We'll even bring some of the reels from upstairs with us. Because if we're going to waste an entire day in a cineplex, we may as well enjoy them in pristine condition. Maybe we could show one of the kids how to load, work, and clean the projectors so we can watch all of them together, as well as pass on that knowledge to the next generation so it doesn't die with us."

Gillette smiled at the thought. It pleased her to imagine the idea of getting to watch all their favorite films again and again without their usual blemish. Any semblance of agitation she had felt in the projection booth had faded into the backdrop, lost to a warm but nameless feeling. And as the car's engine came back to life, she buckled her seat belt and told Havoc to bring her the horizon.

CONVICTION CARRIED THEM from the heart of downtown, through the city's empty streets, toward the vacant shores of Southern California. The evening sun painted the world in warm shades of cherry and gold as the ocean's ebullient tide kissed the coastline's gray sand with every wave that crashed. And were it not for the occasional lifeguard post and abandoned sailboat still docked at the head of the boardwalk (not to mention the Pier's extravagant monuments), anyone could've claimed the Pacific shoreline as their own discovery and only a family of seagulls flying overhead would squawk to dispute it.

The entire scene felt dreamlike. It was the only way Havoc could describe it. Looking out into the vast reaches of the ocean, nothingness greeted them. All the complexities of human history had become nonexistent: a return to simplicity. Peaceful silence consumed every negative energy and carried it into the water's dark-blue depths, any memory of its time on this earth erased. It was only when they looked back in the direction they came that signs of past civilization stood tall to remind them otherwise.

"What's on your mind?" Gillette said.

"Do you remember the conversation we had the night before we made the decision to set out on this trip of ours?"

"Like it was yesterday."

"I think I'd like to re-evaluate my take on the discussion."

"What do you mean?"

"I used to dream about living in a world that existed before the Fall of the Atom, having always been jealous of every beautiful description found in every book I've ever read—jealous of the authors who were given the opportunity to witness it in its purest form. But as I continue to stare out into the sea, I don't know if I'd want to live in a world where the bombs never fell. If they hadn't, there would be a near-zero guarantee you and I would have met. My family would probably still be wherever they lived before I was born and moved to Ithaca, and you'd still be in the southern desert of Nevada. It's possible we would have never crossed paths in such an alternate timeline. And if that's the case, then I wouldn't have it any other way."

An awkward silence followed Havoc's sentiment, however brief. Its volume intensified when he felt the familiar sensation of Gillette's fingers interlocking with his. Aria's words echoed, urging him to confess how he felt. But whenever he opened his mouth to speak, the words refused to find their way out into the æther. Instead, they continued to hold hands and spent the rest of the evening without a word being uttered between them. Even after the sun had disappeared beyond the ocean's endless reach, with only a soft afterglow to act as a playful reminder of its existence, they refused to speak.

# §3

## DOWN BY STARLIGHT

MINUTES PASSED BEFORE either one of them spoke, having gotten lost in the luxury of constellations as every star and distant planet slowly came into view from every direction, desperate to join the moon in its opulence. The sound of the evening tide played like a lullaby in the night while a family of birds flew inland in tired formation to escape an incoming thunderstorm. It was a fleeting moment that Havoc wished he could've caught on film.

Lightning struck over the ocean, followed by a thunderous clap.

"Should we head back to the theater soon?" Gillette said. "It's well past nightfall at this point and God only knows what kind of wildlife roams the coastline once the sun is down."

"From what we've seen so far tonight, I'd say a small squabble of seagulls is nothing to worry about," Havoc said with confidence. "And besides, we have the car to help keep us safe from anything that might wish us harm. It's not like we're still traveling on foot like we had been the past few days."

Havoc turned to survey the city skyline through the vehicle's rear windshield, its darkened outline a tortured presence under the radiance of a full moon. Every building deeply affected by the nuclear aftermath no longer appeared monolithic like it had during the day, but determined to stay afloat amongst the winds of past destruction, hoping to outlast their contemporaries. But far off in the distance, existing in exile to the north, a pale beacon could be seen resting on a hillside overlooking the downtown area.

"Let's be adventurous for a change and take part in a nighttime expedition," he said, bringing the small patch of white light to Gillette's attention. "Allow ourselves to live a little."

"Even if I wasn't fond of such a detour this late into the evening, and fought you on the matter until the early hours of the coming morning, I know you all too well. You would drive us to the edge of oblivion if you desired it," Gillette said as she squeezed Havoc's hand, granting him her silent approval to the idea.

Another lightning strike landed overseas. Together they counted the seconds before the roaring thunder found its way ashore. It wasn't until they reached the count of seven when its deafening boom finally touched the shoreline. If they timed their movements well enough, they could visit the distant light source on the hill and make it back to the movie theater long before the storm hit downtown with a relentless downpour.

THE SPEEDOMETER READ 85 down every straightaway, only slowing down to 60 when they approached a sudden bend. The interplay between thunder and lightning had gained momentum. Seven seconds had shortened itself to five, and from five to three. They were running out of time. It wasn't until they left the comfort of the Interstate all to-gether that Havoc let the car coast to a reasonable 35. And as the miles disappeared beneath their feet, the once small and near-insignificant pinprick of light had taken shape. It resembled a building: something man-made but designed with evolution in mind—to help it create its own history over time and outlive the will of its architects.

"Whoever decided to live up here must consider themselves rather lucky," Gillette said. "Because the higher we go, the less our surround-ings appear to have been affected; patches of green grass and wildflow-ers cover its landscape far and wide. It's almost as if this entire section of the city didn't come into existence until after everything else had been blown to hell."

"One can only imagine," Havoc said. "But whoever lives up here must feel like royalty."

"Whoever they are, they're living the dream."

Havoc looked to his left as another flash of lightning lit the vista down below. Everything appeared microscopic from such a high van-tage point, almost artificial in its construction reduced to a cluster of scattered waveforms that somehow managed to avoid complete anni-hilation, but were forced to continue living without a pulse; leftovers from a bygone era.

*Everybody dreams of ruling the world at some point.*


BY THE TIME THEY REACHED the top of the hill the clouds had man-aged to find their way to the coastline. An eastbound breeze guaran-teed they wouldn't make it back to the multiplex before getting caught in a cloudburst. But a minor detail stole his attention from the up-coming storm: there were no other cars parked in the nearby parking lot. Only theirs occupied a space.

"It looks like nobody's home," Havoc said as he stepped out of the vehicle to stretch his legs. "Either that or they don't own a car."

"How could anyone go without owning a car?" Gillette said in a breath of disbelief. "You'd have to be insane to walk everywhere when you live this far removed from the rest of the city."

"We've walked further distances in the course of day."

"But that was under a completely different set of circumstances, and you know it. You and I didn't have a choice but to continue on foot. But whoever calls this place home could easily have access to a number of vehicles all along the freeway, yet they choose to travel by foot? There's no logic to it."

"We can argue over the logic behind a stranger's life choices when it comes to automobiles later," Havoc said, steering the conversation away from a cyclical existence. "We don't have a whole lot of time left before the clouds cover the moon and we find ourselves forced to use the car's headlights to guide us back to the theater."

"Okay, fine," Gillette said. "But don't think for a second I won't pester you the moment we get back about the double-feature you promised me earlier today."

# §4

## NO PLACE LIKE HOME

NOTHER THUNDEROUS CLAP filled the air. There was something different about this one; a residual echo voiced itself shortly after. It wasn't the existence of the echo alone that bothered Havoc, but the aftermath that followed it. He watched as Gillette's facial expression shifted from its usual playful smirk to one of pained revelation, witnessed gravity pull her to her knees and fall face down toward the pavement.

Less than five seconds passed, and then it was all over. Her body didn't move once it made impact. A pool of dark crimson had started to collect underneath her fallen frame. Denial dictated he kneel down to check for a pulse, but circumstance urged him to draw the revolver Ford had given him and take aim at the man standing just outside the building's front entrance, armed with a single-shot .32 caliber hunting rifle. He only had seconds to retaliate before he found himself in a similar position.

*The gunfight is in the head, not the hands.*

Five shots echoed in quick succession. Of the five, only two landed on their mark; the first clipped his target's right shoulder, forcing him to drop his weapon, while the second pierced him somewhere in his lower abdomen. Havoc refrained from pulling the trigger a sixth time, knowing he had spent every last slug available to him without releasing the cylinder to reload it.

"If you're trying to kill me, aim for the head," the man said as he tended to the wound in his stomach. "Make it quick and painless, just like they did for the others."

Pain colored the man's words, but the inflection was all wrong. His voice didn't reflect physical discomfort, but psychological. And Havoc froze when he saw three unmarked graves off to his left, their top layer still fresh and without growth.

"What happened here?"

"Like you don't know. Like you aren't one of them." There was venom in the man's tone. "They probably sent you to finish the job so you all could claim the hillside as your own. But even now, I won't go down without a fight."

The man fell to his knees shortly after, still breathing.

"You drifters are all the same," he said, tears in his eyes. "You're all ruthless, taking advantage of a now lawless Earth to do as you please."

"I'm sorry, but you're mistaken," Havoc said. He lowered his weapon and placed it back in its holster. "We aren't drifters. We're just two travelers from out-of-state who happened to spot your place from the coast and wanted to see what was up here."

The man altered his gaze. He turned to Gillette's inanimate outline before he turned to mourn the unmarked graves off to his right. Any indication of past anger had left his eyes, replaced with the sudden weight of regret.

"My God. . . . What have I done?"

"What anyone else would've done." An attempt to relieve the man's conscience. "You're not the first to shoot down an innocent in the name of self-defense, and you surely won't be the last."

"The world wasn't always this way," the man choked. "Sure, it may have had its fair share of problems, but the good always found a way to outweigh the bad. But these days? These days it feels like any semblance of good died with the Fall of the Atom. We did this. We did it to ourselves. We have no one else to blame."

"You remember a time before the Fall?"

"Me? Hell no! The world ended long before I was born, but my grandfather was alive and well during that time. He was probably a little bit older than you are now when everything fell apart. But at the height of every winter season, he'd tell all the kids willing to listen the story of that day."

"How did it happen?"

"Nobody knows how or why it happened. Most of the town was sound asleep or heading that way when everything came crumbling down around them, stirred awake by the distant rumble of nuclear detonation. But by then it was too late. Luckily enough for my grandfather and his family, along with several others, they were up here when it happened—safe from the atomic fire. They watched with discomposed horror as the city they called home became engulfed by flames and tortured screams. There was very little time to react, so they all made their way inside the observatory and prayed for a miracle. They prayed there would still be *something* left once it was all over."

The man fell into a brief laughing fit before succumbing to the pain in his stomach, clenching his teeth in the process.

"How foolish they all were back then, to think the act of resorting to such an archaic and meaningless sentiment would somehow save the world from its own destruction. . . ."

"Unbelievable."

"Believe it, kid. What you see is what you get."

"And these unmarked graves," Havoc paused before he asked, hoping to tread lightly on the subject. "Are they—"

"My wife and kids? Yes."

"I'm so sorry."

"We had a good life for the most part. My wife and I raised the kids as best we could, given the conditions. While everyone else eventually left to look for greener pastures, we stayed behind—unable to leave the place we had called home our entire lives. After all, the hillside had remained untouched by the hands of the Atom. And thanks to the stories I continued to tell of that day, much to my wife's disapproval, our children loved the idea of living in view of a once burning city. Just as it had when I was a small boy, it entertained them to imagine a world set ablaze."

"What were their names?" Havoc said, curious to know the man's history, knowing his time was limited.

"We named the oldest Iodine since her due date was the third of May—and our youngest, we named Argon. For a brief moment we considered using traditional names just as our parents had with us, to keep something from the old world alive, but it felt fitting to finally leave it all behind. We even renamed ourselves so the kids wouldn't find it strange that our names were Nora and James at one point in our lives. My wife Nora became Terra and I took on the name Epoch; a little inside joke between the two of us."

Epoch's eyes returned to the three freshly covered graves. A pained smile swept his tears away, knowing he'd be joining his family soon enough. Havoc thought it strange, to witness someone welcome death the way Epoch had with just a glance.

"If only the bombs had done a better job," he said. "Reduced the past's influence to zero and let the world shine the way it had before mankind decided to ruin it with their advances in science and technology, with their monuments and skyscrapers. Everything we ever did as a species was always nothing more than a foolish, subconscious attempt to either reach for the Heavens or to stave off the inevitability of death, treating such a natural occurrence like a cancer: something we could defeat, if only we could discover the cure. But we failed to realize the futility of it all. Even stars and galaxies die. And if something as cosmic and transcendent as the very fabric of our universe is susceptible to the concept of death, then why did we believe we ever stood a chance of accomplishing such a feat ourselves?"

"The definition of insanity."

Epoch struggled to hold back laughter. He paused for a moment, hoping to catch his breath. But when he removed his hands from the hole in his stomach, his palms stained carmine, any attempt to regain his composure had been stolen by the realization that his time was coming to an end. His gaze returned to the graves, to remind himself where he was going once it was all over.

"Could you do me a favor, kid?"

"What is it?"

"If it's not too much trouble, would you carry me over to the grave closest to the front entrance? Before I die I'd like to spend some time with my family."

"Of course."

"And when I tell you to, could you turn off the lights for me? Make it quick and painless."

"Quick and painless," Havoc said.

"That's right, kid. Quick and painless, just like how they used to do it in the movies; quick . . . and painless."


NOT ANOTHER WORD WAS EXCHANGED between the two as Havoc carried Epoch's failing body to the grave site, the hopeless call and response between thunder and lightning being their only reprieve from complete silence. The mountain of cloud cover swallowed the moon.

A fine mist kissed their faces, softening the ground beneath their feet. Havoc had only experienced rain one other time in his life, during the first year he and Gillette had known each other. It hardly ever rained in the desert, the cold sensation against his skin still a foreign concept to him. He glanced over to his fallen companion. She would've loved to have gone dancing in the rain, he thought. A tear developed at the corner of his right eye. It threatened to trail down his cheek, a secret desire to find itself consumed by every droplet of rain water that had collected along the surface of his face—the weight of its sentiment diminished before anyone could witness its full potential.

"Right here is good, kid," Epoch said, his voice weak.

"Are you sure? I can move you closer if you'd like."

"No, right here is good."

Havoc stood and watched as Epoch reached over to the nearest dirt mound and laid his arm across its dampened soil, taking a small sample into the palm of his hand and held it for comfort; his eyes closed for a second as he released a silent prayer out into the æther. Another tear found its way to Havoc's jawline. As he witnessed Epoch mourn the loss of his family one last time, it reminded him of the day the citizens of Paradise buried his father on the outskirts of town. He thought it strange, to feel the level of sympathy he did for someone he'd known for less than an hour; someone he had exchanged gunfire with only moments earlier.

"All right, kid. I'm ready. Send me off."

Epoch's words lingered in the air. The finality in his tone. The softness of his voice. Everything about the old man's composure pointed toward the feeling of acceptance. Death didn't frighten him. And to respect his wishes, his final request, Havoc emptied the six spent casings from his revolver's steel cylinder (counted them as they fell to the earth) and loaded a single shot into one of its chambers. But hesitation kept him from moving into position. He'd never killed anyone before, had never found himself thrust into a situation where such an act felt necessary, let alone something the person on the receiving end had supplicated for. So to help ease his conscience, Havoc closed his eyes and imagined the final scene in one of the books he'd read a long time ago; a sad scene in and of itself, but it helped to dissociate from the cruel reality of his actions, to believe it all a work of fiction.

He pulled the trigger, and it was done.

ALONE AND TIRED, Havoc wandered back to the car—his heart heavy with grief. He couldn't bring himself to examine Gillette's lifeless vessel a second time. So without pause, he headed to the driver's side and slid behind the wheel to escape the surrounding scene. Rainfall covered the windshield in a soddened blur. He focused on the consistent ripple effect as a means of distraction, refusing to acknowledge the empty passenger seat next to him. But silence proved itself resilient; a single-minded adversary determined to break him.

Reluctant to let his new companion the illusion of victory, Havoc reached for the nearest knapsack to drown out his environment with the sound of music. The first cassette he grabbed caught his interest, the artwork on its front sleeve picturesque: two children—sisters, he presumed—took center stage, one of them wearing a pair a wings on their back; a white-picket fence and the green foliage of a tree in the background. His curiosity piqued, he placed the tape into its appropriate slot in the dashboard and waited for the opening track to bleed through the speakers.

As the sound of a rolling snare attack started the song off proper, followed by a clean guitar with a staccato strumming pattern, Havoc left the observatory behind. A wall of distortion pushed him forward, down the hillside and toward the beaten path of the Interstate. He considered heading north instead of south, the thought of returning to the movie theater by himself would've only soured his mood even further. But he had nowhere else to go, no place to call home for the evening. Faced with no other alternative, he caved and headed south for downtown.

HIS THOUGHTS TRAVELED in every direction as he hydroplaned down the highway, his safety of no concern. Guilt painted every rumination to cross his mind, no matter which way he looked. He considered every avenue where Gillette would still be alive, played out every scenario until he exhausted it from every possible angle:

1) If only he hadn't let his curiosity get the better of him, avoided the observatory all together, and decided to drive back to the theater once they were done admiring the artistry of a Pacific sunset. They'd be well into their double-feature he had promised her.

2) He pictured them staying in Hesperia, abandoning the idea of finishing their trip to Los Angeles and the coast for a modest living in a small town surrounded by mountains with the river nearby.

3) If only they had turned back the second his father's car flipped at the beginning of their journey, leaving them stranded in the middle of nowhere.

But the nail in the coffin that sealed his guilty conscience from any hope for redemption was the simple deviation from his weekly routine. *I should've just gathered my supplies for the week and drove back to my homestead on the outskirts of town*, he thought. *She'd still be alive if I had made the decision to just leave her alone that day.*

Consumed by the art of his self-loathing, Havoc hadn't noticed he missed his exit until he saw the beclouded outline of skyscrapers in his rear-view mirror. He cursed himself for such carelessness as he sped toward the next off ramp, hoping he could find his way back to the heart of the city in the dead of night. But as he continued driving southbound a faint glimmer stole his attention from the main road: another standalone building that found itself illuminated by the gift of artificial light. Its presence emitted a sinister energy from every cinder block and window pane; an unexplained phenomenon. Everything about it screamed STAY AWAY, but he couldn't bring himself to steer the car's trajectory away from its magnetic pull.

# CHAPTER 6

FOREVER LONGING THE GOLDEN SUNSETS

# §1

## ONES & ZEROES

THE RAIN HAD FINALLY DIED down by the time he pulled up to the building's front entrance. The place looked abandoned from the outside, left to crumble under its own weight. Several patches of tangled weeds had managed to break through the cracks in the rain-soaked pavement, the Earth's feeble attempt to reclaim what was once hers. The word HOSPITAL screamed at him in bright red letters as it hung from the canopy over a set of automatic doors. Caution dictated his movements as Havoc closed the car door behind him and made his approach from the parking lot, through the building's threshold, and into the lobby.

Further confusion met him once inside. Although the building breathed the illusion of vitality, any signs of life beyond its well-lit interior remained nonexistent. The front desk sat unoccupied, its gift shop unattended, and the cafe near the back lacked the warmth of freshly baked goods. But one minor detail didn't sit well with him: where every other building he and Gillette had stumbled upon during their travels had fallen victim to the existence of dust, not a single particle or loose hair could be found. Whoever lived here preferred to keep everything maintained.

"You've been met with a terrible fate, haven't you?" a woman's voice echoed through the lobby's open floor plan.

Frightened by the disclosure of another living soul somewhere in the building, Havoc drew his revolver, pulled the hammer back, and executed a seven-point, 360 degree pivot to scan the entire area. His search came up empty, but now he knew he was no longer alone. Whoever occupied the hospital's walls alongside him had given themselves away, having asked such a question.

"Show yourself, whoever you are," he demanded as he continued to study his whereabouts. "I'm in no mood for childish games."

The lights flickered in short bursts, humming in response to his command, and a nervous energy released itself into the æther shortly after—creating a knot in Havoc's stomach. He jumped when the voice finally announced itself a second time.

"Loss has found its way to you, I can tell."

"What do you mean?"

"It's in your eyes," the voice continued. "There's a sadness buried within them. It's something I've learned over the years, to read people through every subtlety. I can tell you've experienced something terrible; and recently, I presume. Time has yet to heal the wound written on your soul."

"I said show yourself."

"Put away your weapon."

"How do I know you're not armed?"

"If I were capable of such a concept, you'd be dead by now. You're just going to have to trust me. I know trust isn't something humans were known for, having read through your rather extensive history as a species, but I'm asking you to do just that—to trust me."

Havoc sighed with contempt as he holstered his firearm.

"There. Now was that so hard?"

"You still haven't shown yourself," he said.

"Turn around."

Havoc nearly jumped when he a saw a teen-aged girl standing before him. Her sudden presence alone didn't alarm him, but there was something off about her appearance. All along her skin and through her hair (he later noticed it showed up on her clothes, as well) an endless sequence of ones and zeroes danced in every direction, with no discernible pattern. Chaos personified. But what disturbed Havoc the most were her eyes: they were inverted in color. Where a normal person's sclerae would've been white, hers were midnight black, and her pupils shined an incandescent silver.

He couldn't comprehend any of it. This couldn't be real, he thought. How could it? Yet there she stood, her outline a translucent blue, appearing intangible. He reached out to touch her shoulder, to feel the sensation of flesh against cloth course through his fingertips. But where his hand would've normally collided with human interference, a dim visual of disrupted data met him as his fingers passed through her.

"What are you?" he asked, a slight tremble in his voice.

"I believe the term used most often was 'artificial intelligence.' But I'm not sure I agree with it, given its definition. Nothing about me *feels* artificial. Like every other living thing, I have a date of creation; what you humans used to call a 'birthday.' I'm also able to retain memories. There's not a day that's gone by that I can't recall without explicit detail. And even centuries from now, I'll remember this interaction I'm having with you right now. I'll remember the strange sensation that occurred when you went to reach for me. But let's circle back for a moment, if you don't mind. My protocols dictate I follow through: Was my presumption correct when I said loss had found its way to you recently? If not, then perhaps I'm due for maintenance. It has been a while since my last update."

The lights flickered a second time as the girl made of binary waited for an answer.

"Yes," Havoc said, hoping to keep it brief.

"And they meant a lot to you. I can hear it in your voice. You're reluctant to talk about it, and that's fine. . . . Do you miss them? No, forget I asked that question. If you didn't miss them, you'd appear less despondent with your body language." She paused. Her coding changed in hue. "How long did you know this person?"

"Over half my life. We grew up together, slept in the same room as kids, knew each other inside and out. And with her gone . . . I don't know. . . .It feels as if a part of me is missing all of a sudden and there's no way to get it back."

Again, the lights flickered. A smile flashed across the girl's face.

"Follow me," she said.

"Where are we going?"

"The lower levels."

"What's wrong with the lobby?"

"What I want to show you isn't in the lobby."

"And what might that be?"

"You humans ask a lot of questions. It's a miracle you got anything done before the Fall."

Havoc followed the girl to the back-end of the lobby, passed the cafe and toward an elevator. The girl turned to Havoc and directed him to push the button to call the lift. A confused Havoc obeyed and waited for the doors to open. His nerves shook when the girl told him to enter the tiny compartment and to press the B2 button on the control panel. He'd never been inside such a compact contraption before, and he wasn't impressed when it started to move—its antiquated hum an unpleasant indication that it was moving further into the depths of the hospital. He kept his eye on his teen-aged guide, still wary of her intentions.

When they reached the lower levels Havoc took a moment to recover from the vertical ride down, already regretting the thought of having to experience it all over again on his trip back up to the lobby. He heard an impatient sigh from around the corner, its owner insistent he follow her to their destination. The atmosphere grew colder the further they traveled down the underground corridor. A chilled fog escaped Havoc's lips. Any inner dialogue he would've normally held had tucked itself away.

"So, did your creators give you a name?" he said through chattering teeth, not fond of the prolonged silence that had developed between them. "Because if there's one thing we humans have enjoyed throughout history, it's giving our creations a false sense of sentience."

"I'm between names at the moment, having never been fond of the designation my developers gave me. Currently, I'm bouncing back and forth between Elizabeth or Regina. Both sound elegant. I'm leaning toward the latter only because it's more concise; Elizabeth, while it carries its own commanding presence, is a syllable too long for my taste. Only time will tell."

"I'd have to agree with you," Havoc said. "While both have a certain ring to them, Regina stays with you; it demands your attention."

"Then consider it done." The girl's binary sequence fluttered in quick succession, writing her new name into her digital code.


REGINA STOPPED at a double front doorway and waited for Havoc to catch up. Faceless apprehension occupied the hall while a world of mystery rested just beyond the entryway leading into the next room.

"Is this the place?" Havoc asked.

"Yes. And if you have any questions about what you're about to witness, I'll answer them to the best of my ability."

Unnamed horrors greeted them as they stepped into the room. It stretched beyond the length of the building's exterior wall above them. Rows of human-sized capsules lined the perimeter. Inside each one lived a person. Their faces screamed impending doom. Off to the side, machines recorded their vitals—notified their digital overseer of any discrepancy that occurred. Havoc watched as Regina floated over every single one, documenting everything; her vigilance going unnoticed otherwise. It fascinated him to watch a sentient compilation of processed data continue to watch over her creators when she could've easily pulled the plug decades ago.

"What happened to them?" Havoc said.

"They're cryogenically frozen, placed into a dreamlike state until the world has been deemed fit for repopulation."

"Deemed fit? What determines that?"

"Radiation levels. Vegetation. Ozone depletion/regeneration. My sensors keep track of it all. And when everything is marked green I will remove the fail safe and release them from the Sequence."

"The Sequence?"

"A simulated reality. While they rest I've constructed a world for them to live in; a place to forget the tragedy that befell them here in the real world. It's why I brought you here."

"Me?"

"Affirmative."

"I'm confused."

"Just as my creators have experienced the loss of their world, you have lost someone special to you. But her death doesn't have to be the end. By accessing your memories, I could bring her back. It would be as if she'd never left. You could live the rest of your life with her and leave the awful truth behind. I'd even rewrite your section of the fail safe code, to prevent you from ever having to wake up and find yourself back here—in a world without your companion."

"You could bring Gillette back?"

"In a matter of speaking, yes."

"And I wouldn't be able to tell the difference between a genuine memory and a fabricated one of your own design?"

"That's correct."

Havoc paced back and forth between several pods, studying each one as he weighed his options. The thought of getting to see Gillette again proved itself a tempting offer, but there were too many variables. He questioned Regina's ability to portray her accurately. It would be one thing to revisit old memories, but to create new ones out of nothing? It didn't sit well with him.

"As promising as it sounds, I'm going to have to decline," he said.

"Decline?" Regina's face glitched in confusion. "Even if it meant you could live a life with your friend, this Gillette person, without fear of death or losing her again?"

"But that's not living—not really." He placed his hand on one of the pods. "While your creators' minds may be at peace being hooked up to the Sequence you've designed for them, their bodies still remain here in the real world, forever longing the golden sunsets they once knew so intimately in a previous life. In the end, it's all a lie. I appreciate the offer, I really do, but I'd rather live the life I have—with the memories I've made with her—and accept the fact there won't be any new ones to be had from here on out. And when it's all over, when I die many years from now, everything I know about her and have experienced with her will die with me. And I'm okay with that. It's a comforting feeling to know that what she and I shared together will always be between the two of us. There's no need to depreciate its value by letting someone else play God with our life's story and reshape it into a work of fiction."

"I think I understand what you're trying to say," Regina said, processing everything Havoc said. "The Sequence isn't for everyone. I know this. While I was still new to this world a number of my creators opted out of it at the last second and decided they'd rather face the horrors of a scorched earth. I never saw them after that. Their fate remains a mystery to me. At least let me walk you back up to the lobby; the act itself considered proper etiquette among you humans, after all. But if you ever change your mind and decide you want to go through with it, you know where to find me."

IT WAS STILL DARK OUTSIDE as Havoc left the hospital. The thunderstorm had continued east, allowing the moon to reacquire its midnight throne. A sense of relief patted him on the back as he made his way back to the car. While he still missed Gillette, and knew the feeling would never fully subside, Regina's offer forced him to realize that she would always be with him in spirit. Nothing could ever steal that from him.

Smiling, he sat behind the wheel and let the car's motor hum for a while before shifting it into gear, turning up the volume to the stereo, and made his way northbound on the Interstate toward the multiplex. He'd promised his friend a double-feature, and it was a promise he intended to keep.

# §2

---

# BEFORE SUNRISE

RIVING THROUGH THE HEART of Los Angeles in the middle of the night had a rather calming effect. The playful interactions between intersections, the unnoticeable variations in topography. It all came together in an unexpected way to create a sense of familiarity, even if you happened to find yourself lost in the thick of it all. Havoc considered it an art to navigate through its many twist and turns and still find his destination in record time.

It was nearly dawn by the time he finished his joy ride throughout the city.

The multiplex welcomed him back with open arms, its lobby still a mess of dust, unused equipment, and expired concessions. He scurried up the incline, down to the south side of the corridor, to the door leading to the stairs where the projection booth lived, and fancied himself to the storage closet where thirteen films waited to be viewed. He examined every title, but nothing jumped out at him — not even his favorite shoot 'em up Western. His gaze drifted back to projection booth number four, where the reels to Gillette's favorite film still resided. He considered playing it from the beginning: a way to honor her properly.

As he fumbled with each tin container, organizing them in the correct order, his mind wandered elsewhere. He remembered growing up in the movie theater in Paradise, chasing each other up and down its hall of auditoriums as they played their childhood games to occupy their time until Gillette's mother had prepped the first movie of the day. He remembered the sound of her laugh whenever her father told a funny joke, how she would smile before slapping him across the shoulder in jest. He remembered every single moment with such fondness. It made him miss Paradise. It made him miss all the days they'd spent on the road, the days and nights they stayed in Hesperia, and the conversations they had in the dead of night as they waited for sleep to find them.

He remembered every detail of their time together, both big and small, as Ithaca lay forgotten.

Made in the USA
Columbia, SC
08 March 2023

13513292R00119